CW00557433

RIBBONS

Emmy Ellis

Chapter One

She hadn't killed him, but to someone watching, it would look like she had. In the foetal position on the kitchen floor, Pete Jackson was stone-cold out of it. Unless he was mucking about. Pretending. Waiting for her to come closer so he could grab her ankle like they did in films. But the blood seeping from his head, that could mean he was... No, he wasn't dead, was he? Moments ago, holding a knife, she'd told herself that if he came anywhere near her, she'd kill him, but she hadn't *meant* it. She'd been angry, and people said shit like that all the time when they were in that kind of mood, didn't they? *Didn't they*?

Genevieve Watson backed into the corner of the base units, the sink to her left, the cooker to her right. She'd have to step over him to completely get away, and she didn't have the guts to, not yet. All of her irritation towards him that had built up during the evening while he'd been at the pub, her stuck at home, it melted, leaving her shaking, afraid she'd committed murder. Afraid she'd be caught and sent to prison.

What should she do? Dump his body somewhere? This was her flat, so it wasn't as if she could walk out and leave him to rot. She could go to The Brothers, they'd dispose of him, but...

She thought about the words she'd thrown at Pete, what, ten minutes ago? How she'd revealed her secret in order to get him out of her life. To disgust him so much he'd pack his bags.

'I work for Debbie.'

'Not just any old Debbie. Debbie from The Angel.'

'I'm a prosser.'

He'd thought she worked in a call centre during the day. She'd lied about that for their whole relationship, maybe ashamed of admitting what she did.

'I've been doing it for a while now. Shagged you plenty of times after other men have fucked me.'

That had been the ultimate slash to his ego, the one thing guaranteed to get rid of him, but instead, he'd lunged for her. She'd run from the living room, into the kitchen, and grabbed the knife from the block. Told herself she'd kill him.

Maybe he'd passed out from the wallop to his head, and him being drunk meant he'd sleep it off. What had he said when he'd first walked in, pissed up to the eyeballs?

'Fuck me, someone just chased after me when I left the Seven Bells. A right big bastard with a ginger beard.'

Who was it? What had Pete done for someone to run after him like that? He gambled, she knew that much, and she suspected he'd either been seeing someone else or had indulged in a one-night stand, so maybe an angry husband had come after him. Another woman's perfume on a man's shirt always gave him away, the new lipstick on your collar. Over the months, she'd realised he wasn't the smartest catch she'd ever hauled ashore.

His ex, Zoe, had been a corner girl, too, after they'd split up and she'd found herself the sole breadwinner. Pete had left his debts behind, and she'd had to pay them. She'd given it up recently to work for the twins doing God knew what. Pete had called Zoe all the names under the sun, threatening to tell the social services so their kids got taken away from her, although he didn't want them full-time himself.

Prior to knowing Pete, Genevieve had listened to Zoe slagging him off to the other girls, saying he was a waste of space, a loser, yet Genevieve had disregarded that when she'd met him for the first time one night in the Seven Bells. Pete had seemed nothing like the arsehole Zoe had portrayed him to be, he'd been kind, attentive, an older man intent on caring for her.

All that had changed, and his true colours had slowly crept through until Genevieve had grown to detest him. Tonight, she'd made the decision to end it with him, and look what had happened.

"Jesus Christ." Her bottom lip wobbled, and tears stung her eyes. "Pete, are you awake? If you are, stop pricking about and go. I don't want you here anymore. You can collect your things tomorrow. I'll pack them up and leave them on the doorstep."

She'd get her keys back, too.

She slid the knife in the block. She hadn't even used it, instead reaching for the wooden meat mallet from the draining board, hitting him with it. He'd staggered, slipped on some dirty washing she'd put in front of the machine to sort in the morning, and banged his head on the floor. She couldn't work out if it was the mallet or the smack to the tiles that had his head bleeding. If it was the smack, she couldn't be blamed for killing him, could she? Or would she be culpable anyway because her whacking him with the mallet was what had sent him to the floor in the first place?

"Pete."

She stuck her foot out and prodded him in the side. Air puffed from his mouth. Relief winged its way through her, and she quickly stepped over him, waiting for the ankle grab, every muscle tense. She slung the mallet on the microwave and backed towards the hallway, staring.

He was still asleep.

The doorbell rang. She shrieked, slapping her hand over her mouth. Her heart rate accelerated, and she swallowed to wet her dry throat. She closed the kitchen door and, turning, walked down the hallway.

Who the fuck was here? What did they want? She worked during the day, so none of the girls would have nipped round, not without asking first, and not after eleven o'clock at night. Had Pete told a friend at the pub to come here for a few more drinks? God, the amount of evenings she'd had to endure that happening, her going to bed to get away from them, their loud chatter and laughter keeping her awake.

She peered through the spyhole. A big man stood on the balcony, the light from next door's Victorian wall lamp casting brightness onto his ginger beard. His strawberry-blond hair curled over his ears, and wide eyes stared through large glasses. Shit, was it the man who'd chased Pete? Had Pete been so drunk he'd mistakenly thought the bloke was running after him when, in fact, he'd just been trying to catch him up and was one of his cronies?

She didn't know whether to engage with him or not. He'd go away if she ignored him, wouldn't he?

He knocked again.

Fucking hell.

"What do you want?" she asked, her mouth at the slim crack where the door edge met the frame.

"I need to speak to Pete," he said, voice gruff, low, a Scottish accent.

"What about?"

"Stuff."

"What stuff?"

"He's got some explaining to do."

Bloody hell. Pete had obviously offended him or something. It wouldn't surprise her. He got gobby when he'd had a drink, and going by the state of him when he'd come in tonight, he'd sunk a fair few. Or did he owe this bloke money? Had he borrowed some for gambling? Beer?

"He's not here." She closed her eyes and willed him to go away.

"Yes, he is. I saw him go in, but he hasn't come out."

He's been watching?

If only Pete hadn't lunged for her earlier. If he hadn't, he'd be long gone by now, and the man outside could have spoken to him then, Genevieve none the wiser. But that ideal situation hadn't happened, and here she was, dealing with something Pete had done. Again.

"He's asleep," she said.

"Look, love, you don't know who he is, not really. I just need to have a word, that's all."

"Then have a word at the pub when he's next there." She moved to look through the peephole.

The man glanced either side of him, shrugged, then zoomed closer until his eye filled the lens. It scared her, and she automatically reared back, clamping her lips shut to stifle a whimper.

"Please, leave me alone," she said, her voice wobbling.

"It's George." London accent.

What? "George who?"

"Wilkes. Let me in."

"I don't believe you." She eyed him again.

He partially peeled the beard away to reveal his mouth. "See? Listen to me, he's a nasty piece of work, and I need to… Aww, just open the bloody door, will you?" He stuck the beard back in place.

Relieved she'd have some help, she turned the Yale knob and eased the door open a little. "Why have you got a beard on, and what's the Scottish accent about?"

He sighed. "Long story, one I won't go into. Where is he?"

She stepped back and allowed him to come in. If George was after Pete, it would solve her problem of how to get him out of her place. "In the kitchen." She shut them inside and pointed down the hallway. "Was it you chasing him earlier?"

"Yeah."

"What's he done?"

"What *hasn't* he done?" Ginger George marched towards the kitchen and flung the door open. "Oh. Right." He glanced over his shoulder at her. "Did you do this?"

She nodded. "I hit him with a meat mallet."

He laughed, holding his belly. "Good. I hope it hurt." He faced her. "Are you going to make me a cuppa then or what? May as well make use of the time until he wakes up. Mind you, I could carry him out like this, less hassle."

She walked into the room, hovering by the exit. "I don't...don't want to..."

George bent over and dragged Pete out of the way, sitting him up against the cupboard beside the cooker. "There."

She stared at the blood on the floor. It wasn't as much as it had seemed earlier. She must have imagined more in her panic. "Um, I'll just clean…"

"Give me a bucket of water and a cloth. I'll do that, you make the tea."

They worked in silence, her back to George and Pete, the washing now tumbling around in the machine, and when she turned, cups in hand, George put red cable ties around Pete's wrists and ankles. Thankful he wouldn't be able to get up and lunge for her again, she took the drinks to the little table and sat. George poured pink water into the sink, swilled the bucket out, and threw the cloth in the bin.

He joined her, plonking down and sighing. "What happened?"

She explained, unable to compute that he was really George but knowing he was. The ginger had thrown her right off, as had his excellent impression of William Wallace. She finished with, "I had a knife, but in the end I used the mallet."

"So he took exception to what you do for living, basically."

"Hmm."

"Cheeky bastard. It's an honest day's work, and all money spends the same. I bet he doesn't mind using it to pay for his beer, though, does he. Fucking hypocrite."

"I think it was more his pride. I mean, I did rub it in that I have sex with men then go home and have it with him. I wanted to hurt him, shock him into leaving, let him know there was no going back. I was cruel, but with Pete, you have to be, otherwise he just railroads you into doing what he wants."

"And why do you want him out?"

"He's...not who I thought he was. When he told me he'd nicked money off Zoe, the holiday fund she'd been saving to take her boys away, that was the last straw."

"The last straw? But that was three months ago."

"Oh, you know?"

"Yep. Been biding my time, letting him think he's in the clear. Tonight...tonight I was supposed to let him know he'd been found out, that his behaviour isn't acceptable."

11

"What were you going to do?"

He smiled. "In the end? Kill him."

"Oh God."

George shrugged. "This beard, the wig, the colour, the accent, no one can know it's me, understand?"

She understood all right. He was warning her to keep her mouth shut. And she'd do it. "I won't tell anyone."

"Make sure you don't, else…"

"I *get* it. Are you…are you going to take him away, then?" She lifted her cup, hand shaking, and sipped.

"Yeah, but the problem is, I can't kill him tonight now. I was going to leave his body…well, it doesn't matter what I was going to do, does it, but if I did that, the police would come here, maybe do a few swabs and whatever, find blood I haven't cleaned up. Too risky now. I wouldn't want you getting in the shit. I could dispose of him in the usual way, though, then it'd look like he'd just gone missing, and if you don't report it, no one will come snooping."

She didn't want to know what the 'usual way' was and dreaded to think. "Do you have to kill him? Can't you just warn him or something?"

"Nah, can't be arsed with that. He's upset Zoe and her lads too much. Upset you. He doesn't deserve to breathe." George drank some of his tea then spied the biscuit tin by the kettle. He got up, brought it over, and dug out a chocolate digestive. "Bit peckish."

It wasn't like she could tell *him* off for helping himself, so she smiled and grabbed one herself. Dipped it in her tea, chomped off the damp part. They had five each, neither of them talking, Genevieve imagining what George would do to Pete, whether she wanted him dead or not.

"He doesn't deserve to die, not really," she said.

"In your eyes. In mine... He's broken our rules—and he's enabled someone else to break them an' all, just by being their customer. Did you know he has a gambling problem?"

"Yes."

"We're talking a big problem. An owes-money-to-the-wrong-people problem."

"Shit. Are they...will they come round here, asking him for the money?"

"It's likely. That's why I was going to leave his body on their doorstep so they'd know the debt wasn't going to be paid, but like I said, the blood

13

here…" He finished his tea. "I could send them a picture, I suppose. Of him dead."

"But they might still come round. Ask *me* for it. The money, I mean."

"You can tell them you kicked him out, that if they have a problem, they can go to The Brothers. I doubt they'll do that, seeing as they're running a loan shark operation without our consent. Actually, don't worry about it. I'll deal with it later."

What did that mean? He'd deal with the loan people? She asked him, needing to know whether she should go and stay with her mum for a while in Leeds.

"You won't need to go anywhere by the time I'm done," he said. "Your story is that you two have split up. Last week, say, and he's been staying in the spare room until he found another gaff. Tonight, he moved out, but you don't know where he's gone. Is there anyone likely to miss him? Apart from Zoe and the kids?"

"His mum might phone me, but we don't get on, so that would be a last resort for her. Other than that, there's a few men down the pub. He calls them mates, but they're just people he drinks with. None of them would have his back if he asked for help."

"Have you got any friends who would poke their—"

A groan came from Pete's direction, and George whipped his head that way. Genevieve followed his gaze.

Pete had opened his eyes and squinted over at them. "What the fuck? Jesus, my head hurts." He raised his bound hands to the side of it and rubbed. Stared at his fingertips. The blood. The cable tie. "Did you...?" It seemed he'd properly registered he was tied up and there was a man in the kitchen, a ginger one at that. "Oh, fuck this. What are *you* doing here?" He tried to stand but struggled with his ankles tied and ended up on his knees. "Gen, he's...he's the one who chased me."

"I know," she said.

Pete jerked his head at George. "You'd better get out before I call the police."

"Nah, you're all right," George said in Scottish mode. "Unless, of course, you want to explain to them why you stole seven grand off Zoe."

Pete's expression went from shocked to sly. "Oh, so she's got a heavy to come and sort me,

15

has she? Waited for a while so it didn't look suss? Fucking *typical* of her."

"Zoe doesn't know I'm here." George nicked another biscuit. Munched. "See, the thing is, you've pissed The Brothers off. Never a good move."

"What? I've never done anything to them, so…"

"You don't *have* to do anything to them. You can get them upset by hurting someone else. Your sons, they don't come and see you, go anywhere with you anymore. Was stealing that money worth losing out on time with them?"

Pete grunted. "They'll get over it."

George sighed. "But *other* people won't get over certain things. Like the Weggley sisters."

Pete leant against the cooker, his wrists on the worktop steadying him. "Who the fuck are *they*?"

"Don't dick me about. You know exactly who they are."

Pete glanced at Genevieve as if warning George he couldn't discuss that here. God, she hated him. How he was lying, even now, about not knowing whoever the Weggleys were. Did he *ever* tell the truth?

"That's none of your business," Pete said.

16

"Yeah, it is," George said. "They'll send someone round here to collect off Genevieve. She's innocent in this, but they won't care. They'll want their two and a half grand back. I'd say they were stupid to let you borrow off them in the first place, but a little bird told me you paid the initial loan back with some of Zoe's money, so they trusted you to borrow again. How far behind are you with the repayments? A week? Give it another seven days, and you won't have any kneecaps. Another seven, and you won't have a hand. On and on it'll go, until you're dead."

"Who *are* you, one of their fellas?"

"Nope."

"Who, then?"

"It really doesn't matter. Here's what's going to happen. You're going to die in the end, I just want to make that crystal, but before that, I'm going to clear your debt, and to pay me back, you're going to let me beat the shit out of you whenever I want."

Pete gawped, his addled brain probably trying to catch up, then it did, and he pulled himself up by pressing his wrists to the worktop then jump-walked into the hallway.

George sighed. "I don't know how far he thinks he's going to get with his ankles tied. There might be a bit more blood. Got any bleach handy?"

Chapter Two

George had switched from his Ruffian persona to get Genevieve to let him in, and he cursed the fact she now knew he galivanted about in a ginger wig and beard. He believed she wouldn't tell anyone, she'd be too afraid of the consequences, but still, it grated on his nerves that his secret was out there. He'd told Greg about it recently, but his twin was different, he *definitely* wouldn't blurt it out, but George couldn't worry about Genevieve now. He had Pete secured to metal rings on the wall in his recently acquired lock-up, one he had yet to inform his brother about.

It was situated near the back of the Bracknell housing estate at the edge of a disused trading area that was on the cards for being demolished to make way for one of those poncy shopping villages. A designer outlet, one Greg would love if they sold expensive grey suits and shiny, cost-a-fortune shoes. To get to it, George had to drive along a track between rows of rented garages, something he didn't mind because a vehicle being seen going that way, people would assume he was off to park his car and not think of it as suspicious activity. He left his Ford—stolen by Dwayne, their car thief—behind the lock-up. He'd broken the padlock and added his own lock and key, wanting to use the place for housing Pete until it was time to kill him.

George had agreed with Greg to wait a while before teaching Pete a lesson, but as the days had worn on, George had got arsey every time he'd thought about the bloke. Greg was happy for Pete to be killed, just not yet, but the way George looked at it, the longer Pete walked around, the longer he could treat people like shit. Once George had found out about the Weggley sisters, two weird nutters, loan sharks operating on Cardigan without the twins' say-so, he'd taken a bit of an exception to it. Pete was enabling them to keep working, as were others, and while the usual protocol was to give the sisters a warning, which the twins had done a while back, it seemed they weren't listening. All the Weggleys had done was move their operation elsewhere, going underground as it were, their location now a secret.

Except George knew where it was from following Pete around for the past month.

The twat sat on the concrete floor, chains linking him to the metal rings, and later, when George left him for the night, he'd be injected with something to knock him out, gagged, and maybe, as George wanted to keep him alive for a while, he'd cover him with a blanket. Even in summer, the lock-up got nippy when the sun went to bed.

"Sobered up now, have you?" George asked from an old armchair he'd bought from a charity place. No sense in being uncomfortable while interrogating someone, was there. He'd keep the Scottish accent until it was time to reveal who he really was.

"Fuck you."

George twiddled Ruffian's beard. "You'd better watch your mouth. There's no telling who you're being rude to."

"I don't give a fuck who you are. Anyway, I don't listen to gingers. Did you get bullied at school and that's why you work for those sisters? To make yourself seem important?"

George chuckled. "I told you before, I don't work for them, and no, I didn't get bullied. It's usually me doing the bullying—but only to people who deserve it."

"Oh, and I do? *Yawn.* You're boring me."

People never ceased to amaze George. "You know, for someone who's chained up, you're talking a hell of a lot of shit."

"You'll let me go eventually. I'll agree to pay back the Weggley bitches sooner, and that'll be the end of it. Isn't this how it goes? A few scare tactics, a couple of days in here, and I'll be home and dry."

"Except you've got no home to go to, not now, and I'm not here because of the Weggleys.

Weren't you listening at Genevieve's? You've pissed *The Brothers* off."

"Whatever."

"You don't believe me, do you."

"Nope."

George pulled his beard off, slipped his black-framed glasses in his pocket, and removed the wig. He stared at Pete who gawped and paled.

"I'm George. Not nice to meet you."

Pete's cockiness slipped away, his expression showing his fear, his eyes darting this way and that. "Aww, come on, I'll pay Zoe back, all right?"

"Me and my brother have paid her back, and returning the money isn't the issue anymore. Besides, if you can't afford to pay those sisters, how could you find the money for Zoe? You're full of bollocks."

"Look, if you kill me, the sisters won't be happy."

"Well, no, because it means they lose out on your repayment and the interest, but as I said, I'll clear your debt."

"No, it's not that. I work for them."

George laughed. "Pull the other one."

"It's true. Every customer I send their way reduces my bill. They've got these fellas on their books, two big bastards, they are. They'd give you a run for your money in a fight. I wouldn't upset them, so you're better off letting me go."

George rubbed a palm over his cheek to loosen the stickiness left from the beard glue. He wasn't bothered about leaving DNA behind as he'd be torching the lock-up in a couple of days. With Pete full of enough sedative to keep him quiet for hours at a time, and no one coming by to hear him, there was no reason to worry.

"You've got a good imagination." George stood and walked over to an upturned crate that served as his murder table, like the one in the warehouse. Instead of having his tools lined up on top, they were in a locked briefcase, one Pete couldn't reach, but George would take them with him every night regardless.

He opened it, selected a scalpel, and turned to smile at Pete.

"We had tagliatelle for dinner the other night. Greg's a good cook, he even made the white sauce himself from scratch. Bit of butter and flour, milk, and parmesan mixed in. A roux, he called it. Anyway, we had it with the pasta, and as I was eating, I thought, 'These are like ribbons.' And I said to myself, 'I wonder whether cooked skin would look like this if I cut it off someone in strips, scraped the fat and flesh off, and lobbed it a pan of boiling water."

"'Ere, hold up…"

"Would it be like pork rind? That can go a bit tough. Then I reckoned it would go like bacon rind if it was shoved in the Ninja. Ever used one of those? Greg bought one last week. Amazing gadget. What I'm saying is, I've got a very dark imagination, and there's umpteen things I could do to you to make you suffer. I don't have to beat you up or give you a kicking. I could just slice ribbons off you."

"You're sick in the head."

"I'm not disputing that."

"I'll scream the place down. Someone will come and get me." Pete stuck his bottom lip out.

"How will you scream with no voice?"

"What are you going to do, cut my tongue out?"

"That's an option, but nah, I won't do that." George paced, holding the scalpel beneath the ceiling bulb to press home his point. He'd filled the gaps around the lock-up door with black draught excluder flaps so no light shone outside, and even if someone came investigating, there was always his gun. He didn't mind shooting the odd nosy parker, especially as anyone coming down here would be up to no good anyway. Scum.

Pete wasn't quite getting it. He had an air of arrogance about him again. The fear he'd experienced upon seeing it was George behind all that ginger had faded now, as if he didn't sit on the floor of a scutty lock-up with one of London's most feared people standing in front of him with a scalpel.

Defence mechanism? Maybe. A prick move? Absolutely.

George approached him, kicked him in the head, pulled him onto his back until the chains were taut, then knelt, straddling him. He pinned Pete's arms to his sides with his knees and gripped his throat with one hand. Squeezed, thinking of the drug buyer Ruffian had killed, how quickly the man had gone unconscious.

Pete struggled, bucked, but he went under just as quickly. George shifted back to get comfy then bent and placed the tip of the scalpel blade at the top of Pete's cheekbone. He dragged it down to the jawline, momentarily having the thought that Ruffian was ten times worse than his other side,

Mad George, and he needed serious help. He shrugged it off, because going down that route brought on memories of Janet, his therapist ex, and he didn't want that.

He drew the blade down again, creating a strip half a centimetre wide, then sliced the top and bottom, peeling out a human length of tagliatelle. Held it up to the light. Admired the red flesh on the back, the blood dripping from it onto Pete's chest.

"Hmm."

George got up and hung the strip from a piece of string he'd put up previously, using a clothes peg to secure it. He took a syringe from the briefcase, one of many already filled with the sedative, all of them neatly held in place by the elastic pen holders in the lid. He jabbed Pete's leg through his jeans and let the liquid flow into the man's muscle. Finally, he stuffed a dishcloth in Pete's mouth to soak up the blood. No sense in letting him choke to death on fluid.

The drone of a fly had him smiling, and he glanced across at the hanging strip. A bluebottle had already landed, feasting, and it wouldn't be long before it discovered Pete's wrecked cheek. What had been an idle thought while eating dinner had become a reality, that flies would lay eggs and maggots would hatch.

You could do anything if you put your mind to it.

Chapter Three

Janet smiled at her latest client, Sienna, the air-conditioning working wonders on this sunny summer day. The woman was on the verge of becoming unhinged, that much was obvious, her sobs bordering on the hysterical. Sienna had a busy life, she'd said, living a chaotic, frightening existence she no longer wanted to be a part of. From what had just been said, Janet suspected

Sienna's sister, Hannah, had a touch of George Wilkes about her, someone who could be highly dangerous if Sienna didn't watch herself.

She smiled as Sienna apologised for her tears. Handed her a tissue. Maybe she could fix this woman. Turn her life around. Set her on the right path.

"What would you like to get out of these sessions?" Janet asked. "Do you need someone to vent to, or have you got change in mind?"

"I just need to speak to you when everything gets too much."

"What do you think you struggle with the most? As in, what's the crux of your issue?"

"There was this bloke when we were growing up. Family friend. An uncle who wasn't really an uncle…"

Janet had heard countless tales like this, sexual abuse, and her usual answers sat on her tongue, patient, waiting for the right moment to come out, but Sienna didn't tell *that* story, she told another entirely. Janet soaked it up, sorry for the little girls Sienna spoke about, wishing they'd been born into another family and that life hadn't ruined them.

This was George and Greg all over again, except Sienna and Hannah weren't twins, and they didn't have Richard Wilkes as their father, although theirs had been created from the same mould. What *was* it with these people who had kids and brought them up this way? Why did they think it was all right to allow their children to be used, to fuck up their heads?

If I knew that, I wouldn't be fucked up myself. I wouldn't live, day to day, pretending I'm a stable human being. I wouldn't keep my own issues locked up inside.

Her own issues were another story, though. Today, in this moment, the tale belonged to Sienna. Janet switched her mind off of herself and onto the client. This was why she did this job, to heal, to fix, to bury her mind in other people's problems so they drowned hers out.

Sienna and Hannah now ran the family loan business, their parents dead, both from overdoses, the 'uncle' in a care home, passing his days by dribbling onto his shirt and rocking, something Sienna found highly amusing.

"Serves him right," she said. "Karma did her job there."

"Why does his predicament please you?"

"Because of what he did to me. With *her*. He's evil, and so is she. The pair of them deserve everything that's coming to them. I should have run when I had the chance, got away from the lot of them. I swear, if I didn't know better, I'd say they weren't even my family. Mum let me do whatever I wanted, anything for a quiet life, like she couldn't be bothered to raise me; Dad had a quick temper and shouted a lot, gave me a clip round the earhole more often than not; Hannah picked on me constantly, and as for Abel... Family shouldn't do that to you."

"Do what? I sense there's a specific occurrence that upsets you the most."

"I can't... I don't want to...to talk about it. Not yet."

That's fine. She'll tell me in time.

Sienna sat quietly, staring into space.

The thing that had piqued Janet's interest the most was that the Weggley sisters ran their business right under The Brothers' noses. At one time, Janet would have warned the twins what was happening, but these days? No. George had been about to dump her on the last night she'd seen him. He'd forgotten she was a therapist and could spot a hundred different signs and anticipate what was coming just by body language alone, so she'd got in there first, dumping him instead. She hadn't wanted to, had acted as if it hadn't bothered her, but as soon as she'd got into the taxi, she'd let the tears fall.

She'd loved him—or had been infatuated with what he represented to her. She still needed him so much she couldn't see straight, but it was over. Now, she convinced herself she didn't owe him anything. He could find out by himself, which he would, going by what Sienna had just said—Janet had been so immersed in her thoughts she'd forgotten to pay proper attention. She went back over Sienna's words and winged her answer.

"So someone has been watching, and one of your employees is worried it's the twins. Are you afraid of them? If you've heard rumblings that a man's been seen hanging around outside your new place of business, don't you think you ought to move?" It was her way of warning the woman, without having to say it outright, to get the hell out before she was caught and killed.

Sienna's eyebrows shot up. "Afraid of them? Who isn't? Anyway, it isn't them, it's some ginger bloke. He could have been *sent* by them, I suppose, but... What I can't get to grips with is these people, these leaders who basically run London, who gave them that right? Who do they think they are that they can stop someone from earning an honest living?"

"But you told me last week it *isn't* honest, that what you do is actually *dis*honest."

"Well, yeah, it is, but you know what I mean."

"I think your talk about leaders means something else entirely. That you're annoyed, and hurt, by someone else feeling as if they have the right to do something—to you. Abel and 'her'?"

Sienna nodded.

Janet switched back to the original dilemma. It was clear Sienna didn't want to go into the 'Abel and her' thing. "So, the business. Going after people the day before their debt is due to be paid off and beating them up isn't sticking to the agreement. Last week, you told me that people only get beaten up if they *miss* payments."

"I know, but Hannah reckons its funny to shit them up, to make sure they don't forget they need to pay the next day."

"Do *you* think it's funny?"

Sienna sniffed. "No, I never have. I mean, I'm supposed to laugh, to act like it's hilarious, but deep down… Look, you asked me what the crux of my issue was, and it's that I can feel myself being drawn deeper into the life my parents led, being them, like Hannah is, and I want to stop before it's too late."

"What do you want to do instead?"

"Be one of those respectable money lenders, you know, with a snazzy office an' all that, where I put suits on and have posh handbags. Not this thug shit we've currently got going on."

"Wouldn't that mean people wouldn't be scared of you anymore?"

"Yeah, that's the point. I don't *want* people to be scared. I'd run a nicer business, where I come over all mysterious. None of this beating people up with hammers and whatever. I want to come across the same as Alice in *Luther*. They'd be wary of me, but… God, I don't even know what I'm on about."

Oh dear. "So you want to come across as a psychopath, then."

"*No*, nothing like that. You don't understand, so what's the point of me coming here if you don't even know what I'm on about?"

"I do. You want to put aside the old you—correct me if I'm wrong—and come across as more cultured."

"That's it."

"Why don't you, then? Get yourself a nice office, register the business and be legitimate rather than dealing under the table, and buy those suits and handbags, act the way you want to be perceived." *Like I do, day in, day out.*

"Hannah won't have it. If I said to her I'm going it alone, she'd say I was abandoning her—she always says that. What am I supposed to do with that? She's emotionally manipulating me."

"Why can't you run your business your way and she runs the current one her way? I don't see why that isn't possible."

"Because she'll say we're rivals, that I'm taking away her custom. And she'll hurt me like she always does."

"How?"

Sienna rose and lifted her T-shirt. Scores of scars marred her belly, knife marks. "She's off her tree, and I don't know what to do about it. I told her I was coming here to speak about our childhood, to get some demons put to bed, and I thought it would make her want to come an' all so she could see she's nuts, but she told me I'd be wasting my time. She needs *help*. Tell me what to do. I'm worried she'll go too far and kill someone eventually."

"So neither of you have done that so far?" Janet held a hand up to stop Sienna from talking. "I won't tell the police. What we talk about in here is confidential. I'll only have to inform the authorities if you tell me you're actually going to commit a crime."

"There was this one bloke, old Robertson…"

"That's a past crime. And how am I to know you're not lying about it? Do you understand what I'm saying?"

This had all the markings of her therapy conversations with George. Janet was a hypocrite, preaching to him about the wrongs he committed, yet here she was again, willing to ignore criminal transgressions if it meant she could fix the people who came to see her.

Fix them because I can't fix myself.

Sienna smiled and sat. "I getcha."

Her accent is so the gutter. Reminds me of who I used to be. "How about doing what I did? Elocution lessons."

"What d'you mean? Are you saying I sound common?"

Tread carefully. "I'm saying you don't sound like Alice."

"Ah, right. Point taken."

"So you're not overwhelmed, let's make a short list of what you can achieve this week." Janet folded the page of her pad over and poised her pen to write. "Tackle things one section at a time. Next week, we can see how this progress has made you feel. Hopefully, it'll be that you're more positive. So, first up, book elocution lessons. Buy a suit and a handbag. Go for an Alice haircut and style." She stared at Sienna's bitten nails. "Get some acrylics, a nice red polish on them. That will do for now."

Sienna hid her ragged nails in the scrunched tissue. "You're all right, you are. I thought you were a bit of a twat at first, but you're not."

What answer was there to that but a polite smile?

"Okay, time is almost up." Janet crossed her legs at the ankles. "Do you feel better now you have a way forward?"

"What's the way forward?"

"You'll go your separate ways."

"But I told you, Hannah will hurt me."

Not if she gets hurt first. I think I'll have a chat with George after all. "It'll be a gradual thing," she lied, "so by the time she realises, it'll be as if she's happy about it."

"How will *that* happen?"

"Trust me." Janet smiled again. "That's all you need to do."

Chapter Four

Valerie sat behind the desk, Bear beside her. They always presented a united front when new customers came to borrow money. That was how it had always worked. The pair of them were known for getting spiky if the debts weren't repaid on time, and they were especially particular when it came to taking on newbies. Under no circumstances could they allow someone involved with Ron Cardigan to discover what

they were doing, so by the time punters got to this stage, they'd been well and truly vetted by Abel, Bear's oldest and most trusted mate. He followed them, listened to conversations in pubs, and discreetly asked questions of friends and associates. He dug and dug until he deemed them okay to be granted an audience.

If a mole slipped through the net at this point, Abel had failed in his job—or the mole was good at pretending. Abel was a strange bloke, desperate for Bear's approval. Valerie had long since realised they had shit in their childhoods that bound them together, but she didn't want to know what it was. They had a reputation of being arseholes, getting into fights in their early twenties, so it didn't take much imagination to know they had secrets locked between them.

She'd gone with Bear back in the day, knowing he was someone her parents wouldn't want her to be with, rough as arseholes, not the type a good girl ended up with. She'd been so bloody intent on escaping the confines of the family home, needing something just for herself, that she'd picked the bad apple. She'd drawn the line at marrying him, content to just be together — because if the time ever came when she had to get out, she wouldn't have the rigmarole of divorce to wade through, although there was Hannah to consider, their daughter. He wouldn't be happy if Valerie took her away.

That was by the by, though. She enjoyed her life, the notoriety, the way people cowered in her presence, even at the corner shop when she was getting her loaf of bread and a packet of fags. She'd earnt the respect of those she dealt with, but she wasn't stupid enough not to know that the respect was from fear. Yes, she loved her life, and so long as Bear and Abel didn't do anything to get them in the shit, she'd stick around.

The snivelling wreck sitting in front of them had been sufficiently frightened by Bear in the past five minutes. He'd listed the terms and what would happen if the rules weren't followed. The woman, Michelle Dagenham, blonde, blue eyeshadow liberally applied, had bobbed her head frantically, agreeing to whatever he'd spewed out. Her nails, bitten to the quick, appeared sore. A lack of money and a pile of overdue bills would do that. If she'd been sent by Ron as a spy, she was a bloody good actress. Those tears looked real.

"How did you find out about us?" Valerie asked.

"Someone who borrows off you."

"And who might that be?"

She provided the name of a lady who'd been with them for many years, a neighbour of hers. Satisfied Michelle was just a tart down on her luck, Valerie nodded to Bear who brought the ledger out, a sign that things were moving to the next stage.

"I know you've already given them to Abel, but we'll need your full name and address and any next of kin in the event that you can't pay."

"I can pay. I'm starting a new job next week. I just need money to catch up on the mortgage and that, things I couldn't afford when I got the sack."

Alarm bolted through Valerie. Abel hadn't mentioned that. Someone who got the sack, who couldn't stay in a job, would be a liability.

Valerie drummed her pink-painted nails on the desk. "Why did you get the sack?"

"A few of us were laid off."

Relief. "That's different from getting the sack. You need to learn to articulate yourself better. I was one shake of the head away from denying your loan. Where did you work?"

"The china factory."

Valerie had heard about people being let go, and a handful of desperate buggers had come to her for loans to tide them over. "Right. How long did you work there?"

"Ten years."

So she's loyal. "What's your new job?"

"Some of us got taken on by the other place, the one that's putting my old boss out of business. Same job, doing the glazing, different place."

"How long have you been out of work for?"

"Three months. No one was taking on staff, but then I saw in the paper they needed glazers at Pretty Porcelain, so I went for it."

"It's surprising how quickly debts add up in that time, isn't it."

Michelle nodded. "It's been hard. I've got the kids to think of."

"Do you have a husband?"

"Yes."

"Why can't he pay the bills?"

"He fucked off with some woman a couple of years ago. Can't find him to serve divorce papers."

And this was why Valerie would never marry. You just didn't know what was around the corner, did you. "So you're the only one your children rely on."

"Yes."

Good. Means she'll do anything to fill their tummies.

Valerie smiled. "How much do you need to get you out of a hole?"

"About three grand. I've written all the bills down, the amounts I owe." Michelle passed a folded wedge of

45

papers over. "The bills are there an' all, for proof an' that."

Valerie looked at them. Smiled again. She wasn't the sentimental sort with customers, couldn't afford to be in this business, but this woman was as honest as the day was long. Several red demands, threats of the debts going to a recovery service. The thought of bailiffs coming to the door must have sent Michelle this way. All told, they added up just shy of the three grand she was asking for. She'd have two quid change for a loaf of bread and a pot of jam, the poor cow.

"Will you be paid weekly at the new place?" Valerie asked.

"No, monthly."

"Why don't we add another grand on top of that so you can get ahead. You've got a month in hand to work. How will you survive in the meantime? You'll be forever in catch-up mode otherwise. Didn't you claim the dole?"

"Yeah, but they didn't pay all the mortgage, just some of it. The amount I got didn't cover everything."

"I see you have a few catalogue bills—what some would consider unnecessary outgoings."

Fresh tears spilled. "People say that, but how am I meant to afford clothes for the kids when I'm so strapped even with a wage coming in? Or if something breaks, like the washing machine?"

"I understand." Valerie totted up the catalogue debt. "How about you take another three grand to clear this lot. You won't have the monthly outgoings to them, then. It appears you're shelling out almost three hundred quid on catalogues. That money would then be freed up so you can buy the things you need in cash. Well, you could use some of it, because obviously you'd have to pay us."

"But that would be seven grand altogether. I can't afford the repayments on that, can I? And the interest…"

"With interest, we can do you a deal over a five-year plan at…" Valerie totted it up in her head and threw a monthly figure at her.

The cogs in Michelle's brain clearly clicked together. "I'll do it."

"Lovely. Bear's already told you what will happen if you default on any payments."

Michelle seemed to rethink her options. "What if I lose this new job? What happens then?"

"If you clear your catalogues and close the accounts, you'll have enough money to pay us even on the social. We come before any other debt—before food, the mortgage, the electric, do you understand?"

"Yes."

Bear nudged Valerie's knee beneath the desk. She looked at him, reading what he was silently saying. They'd been after a new person for a while, just hadn't found the right candidate yet. This bird was so desperate to get a better foothold in life she'd be gagging for extra wages. Cash in hand would suit her nicely.

Valerie leant forward. "Come and work for us. You'd do evenings. As a money collector. Like Provident, going door to door."

Michelle let out a nervous titter. "I couldn't force anyone to pay or nothing like that. I couldn't hit no one or nothing."

"You wouldn't have to. We have Abel for that. All you'd do is write down who didn't pay, and he will give them a little visit. Think about it, the money you'd earmarked to repay us, you could spend it on nice things. Take the kids to the cinema, stuff like that. And consider selling the house, renting instead, because then you'd get that rent paid in full on the dole if your job at the factory fell through."

"I can't find my husband, though. His name's on the mortgage as well, see."

"Abel will look for him. He'll find him, get him to sign divorce papers and agree to the house sale." Then you'll be indebted to us. *"What do you say? Five evenings a week, weekends off. We'd only ask you to do three hours, six till nine. At least then, if you find yourself in a pickle again, the loan payments will be covered because we'll keep the wages we'd pay you."*

Michelle thought about it for a moment. "I could do... My daughters are teenagers, so they'd be all right on their own."

Bear filled in the ledger. "We'll discuss the finer points, then. Get everything clear so we all know where we stand. And if you renege on anything, well, what's a pair of broken legs between friends?"

Valerie rolled her eyes at her sister, Yvette. "What the hell have you got involved with him *for? Bear's going to go nuts."*

Yvette bit her lip. "Then don't tell him. What I do in the bedroom isn't any of his business anyway. I only told you in case someone saw me out and about with a fella. It saves you grilling me on who he is."

"Then go 'out and about' elsewhere. Don't do it in the East End. We can't afford for Bear or Abel to see you. Jesus Christ, you're off your meds, you are."

"I'm not on any meds."

"You know what I meant. That bloke isn't for you. You're too nice to be with the likes of him. The bloody stories I've heard…" Valerie stared around the coffee shop, a bit of paranoia flicking at her nerve endings. She shook her head. "I can't get over this."

"It'll be okay. Me and him don't talk about my family anyway, so your secret's safe."

"Oh, you will. He'll be playing it softly-softly to start, then the questions will come. Men always want to know the ins and outs."

"What does it matter if you've got everything below the radar?"

"True. Have you considered he's using you, trying to find shit out? He's the sort who'll want a piece of the pie, to be in on what we do—he's a businessman who's always looking to expand. We manage fine on our own, thanks, we don't need any help."

"Bloody hell, all I'm doing is going out on a few dates. It's not serious."

"Make sure it stays that way. Sleeping with a man like him, where are your morals?"

Yvette shrugged. "The same place yours are. Don't get all holier than thou with me. It's not like you're living a picture-perfect existence, is it. Fucking hell, Bear's an arsehole, you beat people up if they don't pay on time."

"I don't beat them up, Abel does."

Valerie wasn't about to tell her what else Abel did. He had a penchant for using a knife on people's stomachs. It reminded him of the time he'd done something to his wife—a now-dead wife—and he liked to relive it when he could. His go-to method of warning people missed payments weren't on was to give them a little slice. Watch the blood flow.

"He's a weirdo," Yvette said. "I don't get why you've got yourself tangled up with him."

He was a weirdo, there was no denying it, and when Valerie had questioned Bear's sanity when he'd asked him to join them in their venture, he'd made a valid point. They couldn't start up the loan business without him. Abel had a lovely life insurance policy that had paid out from his wife's death, and they'd needed some of it to get up and running.

She sighed. "He's Bear's best friend."

"I know that, but come on. He's creepy as fuck."

"We wouldn't have a business without him."

"But you've paid him back now, you can do this by yourselves."

"What, you're suggesting we drop him? The amount of shit he's got on us... And he could go to Ron Cardigan and spill the beans. No, I don't trust him, not like that. Abel stays. And besides, there's no *way Bear would drop him. They're thick as thieves. This conversation isn't about him anyway, it's about you. Be careful, got it? I won't say a word to Bear; this relationship of yours could fizzle out soon, so what's the point in upsetting the apple cart? You'll be dumped, you mark my words. He won't stick around for long. The minute he gets bored of you, he'll be off."*

Yvette shrugged. "I'll grab what I can get for now. No man has ever taken me Up West, and he does. I like the shows, the nice dinners."

Valerie supposed things would work out okay in the end. The man in question wouldn't keep Yvette as a mistress, he was too tight-fisted to install her in a love nest, to pay all her bills. It would peter out, she was sure of it. In the meantime, she just had to hide it from Bear. He'd go off his nut if he found out Valerie had been keeping secrets, but she didn't trust that Abel wouldn't get wind, then he'd hurt Yvette for seeing someone who could potentially bring trouble to their door. Valerie couldn't risk that happening. Her sister might get on her tits and make stupid decisions, but she was still the only family member she had left.

"Be careful, understand?"

Yvette nodded. "I will."

Chapter Five

Genevieve stood on the pavement and nattered to Tracy, the only corner girl to service men down an alley, never getting into cars. She had a daughter to think of, to stay alive for, she'd said, and at least in the alley she had a chance to get away if any punters turned funny. In a car, not so much.

The sun was being a bastard, bringing on a sweat, and Genevieve was thankful she'd put liquid talc on her inner thighs this morning. It promised to be even hotter later, so they'd all congregate beneath the nearby tree and get some shade come noon.

"So does Zoe know you've split up with him?" Tracy asked.

Genevieve shrugged and completed her lie. "Dunno. He took his bags and didn't say what he was doing or where he was going, and I don't care."

In reality, George had taken everything Pete owned last night after knocking him out again and putting him in the boot of a car. Genevieve had cleaned up blood from Pete's nose breaking, using bleach, and she'd given George the mallet, the cloth from the bin, and prayed no one would come round asking if she'd seen Pete recently.

"I don't blame you." Tracy grimaced. "He sounds like a right tosser. I don't know Zoe, I didn't work here when she did, but it sounds like she had the right idea in splitting up with him an' all."

"He's a waste of space, and I'm well shot of him. He's probably scuttled back to Mummy.

Either way, I got my keys back off him, but I'm getting the locks changed today anyway."

George was sending someone round this afternoon. Genevieve had given him Pete's set of keys so the workman could get in; she didn't trust that Pete hadn't made copies and stupidly handed them to someone. Probably a paranoid thought, but you never knew with him.

"Men, eh?" Tracy sighed.

"I'm staying single for a while. Can't be doing with the hassle."

A man appeared on the opposite corner, partially hidden by a bush. A ginger man. He gestured to her, then disappeared.

"Ooh, there's one of my customers," she lied. "Best be off."

Genevieve crossed the road, making a show of using the app the twins had commissioned so it looked like her movements were being logged. It was for the girls' safety and put her mind at rest that if any of them went missing, at least there was a record of which customer they'd gone with. Punters now had to give names and phone numbers that were kept confidential. If they didn't join the scheme, they weren't welcome on the corner.

"Have fun!" Tracy called after her.

"Not likely," Genevieve threw over her shoulder, "but needs must."

She followed Ginger George down the top of the T section of the road. He got into a different car to the one he'd had last night, and she slid into the passenger seat, noting the tinted windows. Was there a reason for those?

George pulled away and didn't speak until he'd passed the turning that led to the street of shops. "He's not dead yet, if that's what you're thinking."

"It did just cross my mind, yes. What have you done to him?"

"You don't want to know, but let's just say I tore a strip off him last night, and this morning, I did it again. He's ever so sorry, but it's too late. He's asleep now."

"Where are we going?"

"To the Weggley sisters' office, although office is a bit of a stretch. It's a boarded-up gaff on the Bracknell housing estate."

Her stomach lurched. "What do we have to go there for?"

"You need to hand over Pete's money so they don't come crawling round yours."

"I don't want to. They might remember me, come after me later on."

"There's a wig in that carrier bag by your feet, and glasses. Stick them on, and you'll be golden. We need to get a move on, because Greg's at the dentist, and he'll ask me to come and get him in an hour or two."

She was chuffed George trusted her with his secret, although a little afraid in case Greg found out and had a go at her for keeping something from him. She fished the wig and glasses out of the bag and put them on, adjusting the hairdo by looking in the visor mirror. She had to admit, he'd made a good choice. With black hair, she looked really different.

"So what do I do, just go and knock on the door and hand the cash over?"

"Yeah, but they might ask you to go inside. Don't worry, there's also a wire in the bag. I'll pull over in a sec and fit it for you. I'll hear everything that's going on, so if you run into trouble, I'll be there."

This wasn't what she'd thought she'd be doing when she'd woken up this morning. "Can't you send someone else?"

"No. This is between me and you until I let Greg in on it. You're going to tell them he left you and asked you to drop the cash off."

She blew out an unsteady breath through pursed lips. "Right, but just for the record, I'm not happy about it. Shitting bricks, I am."

"It'll be fine. If they give you any gyp, I'll blow their heads off. Just keep that in mind, and you'll be all right."

He stopped and applied the wire, stuck a bud in his ear, then told her to get out of the car, shut the door, and say something to him.

"Can you hear me?" she said, feeling a right twat on the pavement beside a postbox. Anyone watching would think she was talking to herself.

The window sailed down. "Yeah. Come on, the sooner we get this done the better."

Genevieve stood on the doorstep of the boarded-up house, crapping herself. Another one down the way had also been boarded, rubbish and a skip in the garden that indicated it had recently been cleared out. George had parked where he could see what was going on, his seat belt off and the driver's door ajar so he could get out quickly if he needed to.

"Who's there?" came a muffled voice from behind the door. Only the glass had been covered with metal, the same as the windows.

"I've got some money from Pete Jackson."

The door opened slightly, the safety chain taut. A tall blond man stared out at her, his face in folds, as if he had too much skin or had lost a lot of weight. It hung from his jowls, and deep brackets curved beside his mouth. "Did he send you here?"

"Yes. We...I kicked him out, and he gave me this envelope and told me where to come. Said he's leaving London and didn't want to go without paying up." She raised the envelope George had given her.

"Who's that?" someone called from inside. A female.

The man said over his shoulder, "Some tart for Jackson."

"Show her in, then. Don't be rude!"

Genevieve's stomach rolled. *Shit*. "It's here, I don't need to come in..."

The man took the chain off. "Hannah will want it counted in front of you to make sure no funny business is going on. The amount of people who pay with fake notes and think they'll get away with it… In you go." He held an arm out, gesturing to the hallway.

Genevieve swallowed and stepped inside. The carpet had been ripped up, only concrete on show, tufts of underlay in the corners held down by rusty nails. The walls had the remnants of flowery paper, although most of it had been stripped off, the job abandoned before completion. Mould huddled in the top-right corner, its smell thick and cloying. She took a couple of paces in, and Mr Tall closed the door and put the chain back on. Genevieve stood there, a complete lemon, not knowing what to do.

"In there." Mr Tall jerked a thumb at a doorway.

Genevieve went in that direction, her legs going to jelly, and entered the room. A dado rail, thick with layer upon layer of paint, cut the walls in two, black paint at the bottom, dirty white at the top. A teak dining table and mismatched chairs stood in the centre. A woman sat opposite, and another sat at the end to the left. They didn't appear related, their faces completely different, and one had short black hair, the other brown, long, the ends split where it needed a cut.

"I'm Hannah," the black-haired one said. "And this is my sister, Sienna. How did you get this address, off Jackson?"

"Y-yes." Genevieve cleared her throat, nervous beneath their stares. Had they clocked she had a wig on?

"Who are you to him?" Hannah asked.

"I was…we were seeing each other, but I kicked him out."

Hannah roared with laughter. "Why's that, then? Discover he's a knob, did you?"

"Um, he…he stole some money from his kids, and I couldn't—"

"He *what*?" Hannah slapped a hand on the table, a cup rattling in its saucer.

"He—"

"I heard you the first time. Where is he?"

"I don't know. He said he was leaving London and I had to come here and pay you this money." Genevieve put the envelope on the table and stepped back to the door. Being closer to Mr Tall seemed a safer option than Hannah at the minute. The woman looked hard as nails, no one Genevieve wanted to get mixed up with.

"Count it," Hannah said to her sister. "Check it for fakes."

Sienna gave her a filthy glare, drew the envelope towards her, and took the money out. She counted it, then waved some gadget or other over each twenty-pound note. The wait was excruciating, and Genevieve just wanted to get out and run to George's car.

"There's three and a half grand here," Sienna said.

Hannah nodded. "He's calculated the interest. Clever boy. Well, at least he's done something right, but the thing is, he agreed to be a recruiter, so we're going to lose out."

"A recruiter?" Genevieve asked. *So Pete hadn't been lying about working for them, then.*

"Yeah. Bringing customers in. That's all right, you can do it for us instead."

What the fuck? How had this conversation nose-dived so quickly? "Oh, I don't want... I mean, all I'm doing is giving you the money."

"That's what you *thought* you were doing, but things change." Hannah shrugged, as if her word was law. "Are you going to refuse to do it?"

Genevieve wished the wire was a two-way one where George could give advice in her ear, like they did on the telly. "I'm not here for any trouble. I'm just a messenger. My brother's outside, he—"

Hannah smiled wide. "Well, why didn't you *say* so? Get him in here, Finnegan."

Mr Tall left the room.

Relieved she wouldn't be left at this woman's mercy for much longer, Genevieve waited for George to appear.

He walked in, his clothing so different to what he usually had on. Tracksuit bottoms, a hoody, rather than his grey suit and red tie. He put his hands in his pockets and stared straight at Hannah.

"What do you want?" he said in a Scottish accent.

Hannah raised her eyebrows at Genevieve. "Brother, you say?"

"Brought up by different mothers," George said. "What's going on?"

Hannah took the money and put it back in the envelope. "You're a big boy, look like you could be handy with your fists. I offered your sister a job as a recruiter, and it doesn't seem like she wants it, so how about I give her a different job? A money collector. You can be her bodyguard."

George frowned. "She doesn't need a job, she's already got one."

"In the daytime, is it?"

"Yeah."

"Then that's perfect. She can work in the evenings."

It was clear she was used to dishing out orders and being obeyed. How would George react to that? They were birds of a feather, and *he* was usually the one calling the shots.

"No, thanks." George tilted his head at Genevieve, indicating for her to leave.

She went into the hallway, Mr Tall moving aside so she could pass, but he held her elbow and went with her, a warning she had to stay put by the newel post.

"Did you say no thanks?" Hannah asked. "I'm sure you did, or are my ears playing tricks on me?"

"You heard me right," George said.

"Do you know who I *am*?"

"Nope. Should I?"

Hannah laughed quietly. "I'm not sure I like the sound of that. I thought I was more famous around here. Perhaps it's because you come from Scotland, you're not familiar with the people in the East End yet. Hmm, I'll let you off, but in future, don't speak to me like that again."

"Like what?"

"Like I'm shit on your shoe. It won't bode well."

Genevieve held her breath. The woman thought she was a face, someone to fear.

"Why's that, then?" George asked.

"You're rude, and that needs to be punished."

George spurted laughter. "Who are you going to get to do *that*?"

"Finnegan," she called. "Come in here and sort this pleb out, will you?"

A gunshot fired as Mr Tall entered. Genevieve screeched in shock and peered around the doorframe, dreading what she'd see. Hannah cradled a hand to her chest, teeth gritted, breathing heavily through her nose. She stared down at the bleeding stub of her little finger. Mr Tall backed off, hands up, and stood behind Sienna.

"You fucking little shit," Hannah shouted. "You'll pay for that. My finger. You shot off my fucking *finger*!"

"Nah," George said. "I don't pay for anything, and neither does my sister. I'll be kind this time and leave Jackson's money here, but if we get any hassle when we leave, a bullet will find its way into your man's head, and that envelope will be going with us."

"Finnegan…" Hannah said. "You know what to do."

George raised the gun at the same time Finnegan raised his. Another sharp retort, and Finnegan flew backwards and landed on the floor, a hole in his forehead, blood and bits of gore decorating the left-hand wall. Sienna stood, moving to the blocked-up window on the right, and Hannah remained seated, staring from Finnegan to George.

"Who the *fuck* do you think you are?" she screeched, her face pale, likely from pain.

"Never you mind," George said, snatching up the envelope. "Have a nice day."

In the car, George driving casually, Genevieve glanced out of the rear window, her heart beating too fast, her mouth dry. No one followed, so she turned back and stared ahead as he navigated the streets.

"What the hell?" she said.

George laughed. "Fun, wasn't it."

"Fun! *Fun*? No, it was bloody horrible."

"Fuck her and the donkey she rode in on. I did contemplate doing what she wanted, collecting their money, but it wouldn't have served a purpose."

"And killing that bloke did?"

"Yeah. Made my fucking day."

Genevieve shook her head. "What happens now?"

"We're off to the breaker's yard to dump this car, burn our disguises, then I'll take you home in the BMW."

"But they'll find out who I am, send someone to hurt me."

"I'll deal with it. Set you up in a hotel somewhere for the time being."

"You make it sound so simple."

He smiled. "It is."

Chapter Six

Sienna would have stared out of the window if it wasn't boarded up. Not only to see what vehicle those two had arrived in, but so she had a view that could take her mind off Finnegan's dead body. Hannah didn't seem bothered by their man's death, instead screeching about her missing finger down the phone to whoever she'd rung.

This. *This* was why Sienna wanted to change the way they ran their business. She'd *told* Hannah that Finnegan was as much use as a colander when you needed a bowl, yet she'd insisted on using him. Whoever that ginger man was, well, he was far more adept with a gun, better at acting as if no one scared him, and would be a great asset in Sienna's new company.

It must be the same bloke who'd been seen hanging around outside recently. How come Hannah hadn't twigged? Why had he been watching them, though? The woman had said Jackson had given her the money last night, so had he told her brother about this place before then?

Hannah slapped her phone on the table. "We've got to go to the clinic."

"Obviously, because if you go to a normal hospital, they're going to ask questions, seeing as a *gun* was used to blow your finger off. Do you see now, eh?"

"See what?"

"Why we need to change the way we do things? Finnegan didn't even check him for a weapon when he came in. We need to start searching people, not just rely on the fact you think you're some woman gangster no one will cross."

"Don't be stupid. This just makes me want to get bigger guns. A *machine* gun will do the trick."

Fucking Nora... "What are you going to do about *him*?" Sienna gestured to Finnegan.

"Me? Why is it me all of a sudden when you're the one who cleans up messes?"

"Because I want no part of this. I've been telling you to deal with people in a better way, yet you riled that bloke up on purpose, got all shitty because he doesn't know who you are."

Hannah sniffed. "Get all our loan money together and put it in the bag. We can't stay here now."

"So you're just going to leave Finnegan to rot, are you? Are you thick?" Sienna was pushing it with that comment, but for fuck's sake...

Hannah slid her phone in her pocket and held her ruined hand up. "*What* did you just say?"

"Oh, stop trying to bully me all the time, it's boring." It wasn't so bad, standing up for herself. There was no Finnegan to hold her down while Hannah cut her. "Think about it. If we leave him here, someone's going to smell him eventually. They'll blab that we were using this place, and the police will come knocking on our door. We need to get rid of him ourselves, wash all that blood away, and carry on using this house."

Hannah's glower pierced Sienna. "Fine, we'll do it your way. We'll still take the money, though. Anyone could be watching out there and come in to nick it."

"Why do I have to go to the clinic with you? No one's here to watch the place now Finnegan's carked it."

"Fair enough, stay here, but good luck having no security—or *me* protecting you, come to that."

Protecting me? More like controlling me.

Hannah flounced out, the front door slamming. The rev of an engine meant someone had come to collect her, maybe Donkey, her favourite bully boy. Sienna breathed out a sigh of relief at being left alone, although that wasn't strictly true with the dead prat on the floor.

She sat at the table and avoided looking at Finnegan. She reckoned, if she got rid of the body off her own bat, Hannah would go spare when she got back. She always wanted to be the top dog, using Sienna as her lackey, plus she'd want to choose the method of disposal, the location.

Annoyed, because she was supposed to be getting her nails and hair done in an hour, Sienna seethed about being stuck here guarding the money. If she left, she'd get in the shit with Hannah.

She'd have to bring in their other bully boy to babysit.

Sure Donkey was who Hannah had turned to, Sienna sent a message to the other one and waited. Why should her day be disrupted because her sister couldn't control herself? Sienna had plans to look just like Luther's Alice, and she had no intention of letting Hannah derail that. Janet had said to pacify Hannah, to change things around here gradually so her sister wouldn't notice, but it was going to be hard, especially if that ginger man came back and pulled a similar stunt. It wouldn't be so bad if Hannah copped a bullet in the head, but Sienna didn't fancy dying just yet.

A knock on the back door startled her, even though she'd been expecting it, and she went to the kitchen, nervous in case it was that Scottish man again. Hannah had ignored her by not having spyholes installed in the doors, so there was the palaver of asking who was there before they opened up. She glanced around the bare kitchen, paranoid someone stood in the built-in larder, asking herself, not for the first time, why she hadn't left home as soon as she could and got away from not only her parents, the weird uncle, but Hannah as well—and this life.

At the door, she called, "Who's there?"

"Two-Time, who d'you think?"

She swung it open. "You know we have to ask."

Two-Time stood in the garden, smoking a rollie, black hair slicked back, double scars down the side of his face from the two times he'd been slashed, hence his nickname. Thick-set, he looked menacing but was quite a nice bloke underneath the scowl.

"Where's the fire?" he asked.

"I need you to stay with Finnegan and the money." She wafted a hand so he came in quickly, impatience searing a hole inside her.

"Why can't Finnegan watch it? Or Hannah?" Two-Time stepped inside and shut the door, turning the key in the lock.

"Because he's fucking *dead*, and Hannah's gone to the clinic, that's why."

"What?" Two-Time stared at her, eyes narrowed.

"Hannah got a bit above herself with a bloke, and he shot her finger off and Finnegan in the forehead. Come on." She led the way out of the kitchen and into the living room, standing at the farthest end of the table from the body, arms folded.

"Hannah's had a finger shot off?" Two-Time came in and stared at the bullet hole in the tabletop. "How did she even let it get to that point?" He stooped, picked up the spent casing, the bullet, and slipped them in his pocket.

What's he up to?

"You know what she's like." Sienna pointed at the body. "We'll work out how to get rid of him later when Hannah gets back. She's the boss, so she can arrange things."

"You sound narked with her. What's going on between you two?"

"Nothing." She didn't trust him enough to let out all her gripes, and he was asking a lot of questions which put up her guard. "I've got a couple of appointments, so if you could just babysit him. Maybe don't open the door to customers until Hannah's here."

"How long will she be?"

"How long does it take to sew up a finger stump? Dunno." She remembered what Janet had said and amended her speech. "I don't know. Not sure I'll be back today either. I've had a bellyful, and it's still only morning."

She strode out via the front, thinking that if Hannah thought she was the big boss, *she* could bloody deal with any other shit today. Phone switched off, Sienna got in her car, grimacing at her reflection in the rearview mirror. Her hair was well past time for a cut, so her first appointment couldn't come soon enough. Once she'd had her nails done as well, she'd go to the department store and get them to do a free face of makeup. Then she'd buy a suit and handbag, some fancy shoes. All that was left of her weekly jobs after that were the elocution lessons, and they started online the day after tomorrow.

Not bad, completing her to-do list early.

Janet would be proud of her.

Sienna didn't recognise herself. Hannah would either laugh at her or poke and prod about why she wanted to change her appearance. Encourage her to go back to how she'd been before. Bitten nails, manky hair, no makeup. She'd more than likely berate Sienna, like Dad and Abel used to, trying to make her feel inferior, saying she had ideas above her station. It wasn't that, she was just sick of going around like a skank. Acting like one.

Hannah could go and fuck herself.

Sienna wandered through town for a bit, enjoying the way people stared at her—she did seem odd, her face and hair all nice, yet she had her grubby casual clothes on, leggings and a long T-shirt. She'd been tempted to keep the suit on after she'd been in the fitting room, but too much change at once would set Hannah off. It wasn't as if they couldn't afford to dress up either, they had plenty of money, but Hannah was so invested in sticking to their roots that there was no room for arguing the toss. Well, Sienna wasn't going to sit back and take it, she'd already proved that by having a dig or two at Hannah before she'd gone to the clinic.

She bought a handbag from New Look but kept it in the carrier bag. She'd stash it at her flat. And that was another thing. She didn't want to live next door to Hannah anymore. She needed some freedom. To be able to come and go as she pleased without Hannah keeping tabs. Hannah's promise to their parents to 'keep an eye' on Sienna had gone to the extreme.

She drove home, dropped her things off, then went to the loan house. Two-Time let her in, grumbling that she'd been gone ages and there had been no contact from Hannah, then he noticed what she'd had done and gawped.

"Fuck me sideways. What happened to *you*?"

So he was going to pick on her as well, was he?

"Piss off."

"I don't mean it in a nasty way. You look nice."

That pleased and shocked her. She hadn't been paid a compliment, ever. "I bet you never thought you'd say that to me, did you."

"Well, you two don't exactly make the best of yourselves, do you. No offence or anything."

"None taken." Not much anyway. "I'm tired of it, being grotty, so here we are." She stuck the kettle on the camping stove, seeing as there was no electricity. "Have you messaged Hannah?"

"Yeah. No answer. Maybe she had to be put under or something," he said. "Local anaesthetic might not be enough. Donkey isn't replying either."

"I'll text her now." She turned her phone on, and several beeps blared out. She glanced at the screen. "Oh, she's got hold of me, hang on."

HANNAH: GOT TO HAVE A QUICK OP. GET TWO-TIME TO PUT FINNEGAN SOMEWHERE. GO WITH HIM. I WON'T BE BACK UNTIL TOMORROW MORNING.

HANNAH: ARE YOU STILL IN A STROP?

HANNAH: ANSWER ME, YOU STUPID LITTLE COW.

HANNAH: OH, FUCK OFF, THEN. YOU ALWAYS WERE A SULKER.

Always being the whipping post had Sienna scrunching her eyes closed, tears of frustration burning. Janet had said Sienna had been conditioned to obey, but the fact she wanted to break free showed Hannah's control wasn't as strong as it once was. And was it any wonder she'd sulked since *that* night, all those years ago? What had happened then, and continued to happen if Sienna didn't behave, would send anyone into the doldrums.

I hope she dies while she's being operated on.

Angry at always being spoken to like shit, Sienna reckoned it was about time she fought back. She wasn't a little girl anymore, she was a fucking *adult* and was entitled to stand up for herself.

Sienna: To answer your questions in order... 1) Will do, but only because I can't stand seeing F here. 2) Just a bit. 3) I'm answering you now. 4) Fuck off yourself.

Her stomach rolled at number four, but God, she couldn't keep letting Hannah dish out orders. Her need to stick up for herself overrode the fear of being cut.

She smiled at Two-Time. "Looks like we've got a body to dump. Know anywhere he won't be found?"

He pinched his chin. "Yeah, the same place as old Robertson. He hasn't been spotted yet, so the location's safe. It'll have to be tonight, though, so we don't get seen."

"Obviously." She put teabags in the manky stained cups. "Has anyone been round?"

"Two knocks, but I ignored them."

Courage came and tapped her on the shoulder. "With Hannah out of commission until tomorrow, we may as well lock up, drop the money at mine, then go down the pub, get seen before we dump him. Alibi an' all that."

Two-Time nodded. "People won't recognise you like that."

"We'd best make sure they know it's me, then. I'm not going down for murder just because my sister's got a god complex."

"There's something I wanted to run by you anyway."

The kettle whistled, and she turned the gas off. Poured water into the cups, then added powdered milk and some sugar. "What's that, then?"

He sniffed. "I'm going to be moving on."

You and me both. Is he testing me, seeing if I'll open up to him so he can go scuttling back to Hannah with information? "How come?"

"Been offered a better job elsewhere."

"Oh right. Hannah's going to do her nut, you know that, don't you. I won't tell her, by the way."

"I'm not scared of her, and she knows it."

Sienna wished she'd told him her plans before now so she could have asked him to join her in her new business, but since he had a new job, she wouldn't bother saying anything. "Dare I ask who you'll be working with?"

"Nah, you might accidentally let it slip, and I don't fancy her passing it on to Donkey. She'll tell him to do me over."

"Like that, is it?" She squeezed a teabag against a cup then handed the drink to him. "I doubt Donkey will give a shit what you're doing. With you gone, he'll be her main protector."

"No, it'll do him a favour, but he'll come for me if Hannah tells him to. He does whatever she says, although I sense the worm is about to turn with him an' all."

"Really? I hadn't noticed a difference in him. Or you, come to that. I've had my own issues filling my head."

"Like what?"

"Can I trust you?"

"Of course you can. Jesus, I've just told you I'm bolting, so that means *I* trust *you*."

"Hmm. Hannah could have put you up to it to test my loyalty."

"She didn't. I'm done, seriously. I think you should get out, too, while you can. She's getting worse."

Sienna sighed and squeezed her own teabag. "There's a common denominator here. You,

Donkey, and me, we're all getting sick of her shit. The only one who wasn't was Finnegan."

"Ah, he was after getting in her knickers."

"What?" Sienna laughed. "Who knew. Best you keep everything we've discussed to yourself, then, and *I* certainly won't be telling her. You've heard me pissing and moaning at her lately; I'll be moving on myself before long. She's doing my head in." A sinking feeling hit her. What if Two-Time *had* only said all that to see what she said? What if he *did* report back to Hannah? "Sisters, eh?" She laughed to take the seriousness out of her words.

"Hmm, but she's not your sister, is she."

Did *everyone* know? Had Sienna been the last one to find out? She winced. No, they weren't siblings, according to Abel, but there was still a weird sense of loyalty towards Hannah, something Janet had said would take a while to get rid of. "Shame she lies and makes out we are."

"Get a DNA test done. Then you can get out of the business without her spouting that you need to stick together out of family duty."

"She'd only say family doesn't have to be blood. She has an answer for everything."

"Then come and work for the same people I'll be working for."

"Not without knowing who they are."

He sighed. "I can't tell you unless I have permission. If you don't know, then Hannah can't stab the information out of you, can she."

"How do you...?"

He shrugged. "She talks about it, that's how I know. She brags about cutting you. That's why I went to my new bosses in the first place this morning and asked them for help—for *you*. I can't sit back anymore and let her run riot. She needs to be stopped; she's going off the rails. Did she tell you what she was up to last night? That was the last straw for me."

Sienna thought back to the previous evening. Hannah had gone out, dressed all in black, and hadn't come home until about three in the morning. Sienna only knew that because Hannah had slammed her front door both times.

"Do I really want to know?" she asked.

"You do if you don't want to get caught up in the aftermath, because I'm telling my new bosses soon. They were a bit busy this morning for me to explain everything, so we're meeting up later."

A sense of unease skittered through her. "What did she do?"

"Killed a kid."

"*What?*"

"A little girl. She was eight."

Sienna's knees went from under her, and she sagged against the worktop. "What... Why? What did the poor thing do?"

"She wouldn't open the door so Hannah could speak to the kid's dad. He was three days late in paying her. Hannah shot her through the glass. It's all over the news."

Sienna righted herself and, sick to her stomach, lurched into the living room and picked up the money satchel. This was it, *her* last straw, and she wasn't having anything to do with this business—or Hannah—again.

She returned to the kitchen, hanging the satchel on her shoulder. "Still got that petrol can in the boot?"

Two-Time nodded.

"Then we'll set this place on fire. I don't want my fingerprints being found in here. Hannah's on her own now, I want no part of killing kids."

He tipped their teas away and moved to the back door. "I'll do it. Go. Meet me at the Seven Bells."

She didn't worry about the neighbours. The house was detached. She left, shaking all over, and drove off, scared and angry at the same time.

Yes, Hannah needed to be stopped, but who would be brave enough to do it?

She thought of The Brothers and took a left corner, away from the Seven Bells.

The pub *she* needed was The Angel.

Chapter Seven

Yvette had been seeing her fella for three months, and he still hadn't asked about her family. Maybe he knew who they were and hadn't found out about the loan business. Valerie was right in what she'd said. If he did find out, he'd want in on it. He was always looking for new ways to make money, he'd made that clear on the nights they'd gone for meals and chatted

for hours. He was keen to make his fortune, although he was already loaded.

Maybe that was the appeal for her. His money. The stability it would bring. But she had to face it, there was no way he'd want anything serious with her. She was just a bit on the side, a distraction, a release from his busy life.

Tonight, she'd put on the dress he'd bought for her, dropped round to hers by a courier. Fancy, expensive, shoes to match. He liked her to tart herself up, to look the part of a mistress, although he'd made it clear she wasn't the only one he'd had affairs with—and he'd forced her to promise to keep that to herself. It was their 'little secret'. She supposed she ought to shy away from a man like him, but she hadn't been able to resist when he'd first approached her. Who wouldn't want a rich man to wine and dine them? Being treated so nicely was the only thing she was after at the moment.

She enjoyed the secrecy of it all. The fact that people wouldn't believe her even if she did say she was seeing him. Valerie had, but others, they'd laugh, say she was living in cloud cuckoo land if she thought they'd swallow such an unlikely story. Maybe that's why he'd picked her. She wasn't the type people would expect him to go for. She was way too common for a start. He probably wanted someone who'd be with him without question, do whatever he said.

A horn tooted outside, and she grabbed her bag, checking her makeup in the hallway mirror. He liked her to lay it on thick, said he had a thing for heavy kohl, the look of women in the sixties. So he didn't toot again and get arsey, she rushed out to his car. He had a different one every week. He insisted on going out in disguise anyway, a beard and wig on. She had to admit, it did change him a lot. She wouldn't recognise him if she didn't know who he was.

She wasn't stupid, she knew he disguised himself in case he was spotted with her. Was she an embarrassment, was that it? She should feel upset about that, but she wasn't. When she was with him, she felt desired, and that was enough.

She got in the passenger seat and popped the safety belt in place. He leant over and kissed her cheek, his scent some cost-a-bomb cologne, his suit probably tailor-made in a posh shop. She reckoned the price of his tie alone would pay her monthly rent.

"Where are we going?" she asked, anticipating a nice meal. Her stomach rumbled; she hadn't eaten all day, having held off so she'd have room to fit a three-course in.

"The Savoy," he said and drove off.

"Blimey."

"I want you to play the part of a brass tonight."

He was weird like that, asking her to pretend to be different types of women. He obviously liked playing out his fantasies. While it was odd, so far she'd coped with it, although a brass was bordering on 'no' territory—not that she'd ever be able to say that to him, he didn't like the word no. She didn't have anything against sex workers, she just didn't want to be one, but he wouldn't give her a choice. Valerie would say she was one, having sex at the end of the night after he'd paid for a show and a flash dinner, but Yvette didn't want to think about that.

"An escort," he said. "You know, the high-end type of slapper."

"Okay."

"So the sort who acts the part of whatever the punter wants, then she gives out at the end of the night, but only if he shells out more money."

Why didn't he just employ one of them, then? Wouldn't it be easier? She kept those thoughts to herself but said, "And will you pay me?"

"Of course I bloody will."

That was new. She thought he'd have told her to fuck off on that one. Maybe he needed to hand money

90

over for it to seem real. "How much do escorts charge?"

"The sort I want you to be? A grand just for the pleasure of her company, then another grand for sex."

Her stomach flipped. A chunk of change like that… There was no way in this life she'd get it otherwise. Her job paid just enough for her to get by. She could afford more if she'd taken Valerie up on her offer of being a money collector, but being involved in that business wasn't something Yvette was prepared to do. There were too many risks, too much subterfuge going on. Her rent wasn't much, she still lived in the childhood home, a council house, although there were grumblings she might have to move out as it was a three-bed and too big for a single woman. If she had kids, that would be different, but that wasn't on the cards just yet.

"So are we playing the game as of now?" she asked.

"Yep."

"Then I want the grand for my company."

He laughed. "That's it. I knew you'd get the gist. The cash is in one of the envelopes in the glove compartment. Remember, you do whatever I want, got it?"

She took the envelope out and opened it. "Fine by me." She paused, a thought striking her. "Hang on, I don't get to keep this, do I? It's just part of the game, and I'll have to give it back."

"No, you can keep it."

What? Then her heart sank. Was this a final goodbye? A payoff to keep her sweet when he dumped her later? She'd been surprised he'd been seeing her for so long as it was, so it made sense they'd come to the end of their road.

It had been good while it lasted, and she'd miss the nights out. Him, not so much. He talked a lot about how he managed his workforce, how he made his money, and the majority of his dealings were underhand. He was a businessman who didn't take no for an answer, which was why he was so rich.

She counted the money. A grand in tenners. This would pay her rent in advance, a few bills, and the other grand later, for the sex, she could buy all sorts with it. Clothes, shoes, makeup, that nice handbag she'd seen in the covered market.

She'd be a tart for him more often if this was what she got out of it. Like she'd said to Valerie, she'd take what she could get. One day, all this would be over, a distant memory, one she'd drag out from time to time as an old lady, smiling at how she'd sold herself for a while to a man she couldn't say no to, muttering, "Those were the days…"

She popped it in her bag. "Do I need to have a made-up life? I mean, will we talk about that over dinner?"

"Yeah, so think about who you'll be tonight. By the time we get there, I want you to be her. Let's see. You're called Honey, you're twenty-one, sophisticated, and you make so much money you live in a penthouse."

She warmed to the theme and rested her head back, closed her eyes, imagining who she'd be if she wasn't Yvette. If she could be anyone she desired. It wouldn't be a brass like her friend, Twinkle, that much was certain, but for tonight, she'd play his games. They were fun and took her out of her boring world.

It was better than a poke in the eye with a sharp stick.

The food had been perfect, clearly top-end. He acted as if he'd been here on numerous occasions, and flashing the cash meant they received perfect service, the waiter fawning over him. She wondered if they knew who he was beneath that beard and wig. Maybe not. He'd changed his voice, as he so often did, the roughness of the East End replaced with something smoother.

"Thank you for your company tonight, Honey, but I don't want the evening to end." He winked.

She smiled at him. Winked back. "It doesn't have to."

He relaxed against the red velvet booth seat, the picture of a man who was comfortable with who he was. "Do you provide extras?"

"At a cost."

"And how much would that set me back?"

Honey was the kind of woman who spoke her mind. She'd been trying that out all evening, to see if he pulled her up on it, but so far, he'd accepted whatever she'd said. "I hardly think extras could be spoken of in such a derogatory way. 'Set me back' sounds negative, when all I offer is the positive."

His face clouded. Had she gone too far? Had he forgotten, just for a moment, she was playing a part, one he'd asked her to?

His features softened, and she breathed out her relief.

"Very good," he said. "I almost believed you weren't Yvette, then. So, how much?"

"One thousand pounds."

He reached inside his suit jacket pocket and took the other envelope from the glove box out, pushing it across the table. "This buys whatever I want."

She nodded. "It does."

"Whatever?" he stressed.

Unease prickled her skin. Were they still playing the game? "Within reason. I have boundaries."

"But what if I don't want Honey to have them?"

"Then as an escort, Honey has the right to decline."

"What about as Yvette?"

He was blurring the lines, manipulating it to his advantage. She didn't like it, he wasn't being fair, but then she supposed he never was. It had been clear from the start he always got his own way and she'd have to do as she was told. She'd walked into this knowing if he wanted her, she couldn't say no—he was just that type of man, commanding, demanding, and she'd strutted straight into it for the excitement.

She held back a sigh. "When I'm Yvette, you already know those boundaries."

He laughed. "There haven't been any so far."

No, she'd done whatever he'd wanted sexually. He was a bit rough, too quick for her liking, and he had a habit of gripping her throat from time to time, but it was all fun in the sack, and one of her past boyfriends had a thing about strangulation, so it wasn't new to her. "Then that answers your question, doesn't it?"

"No. There are so many things we haven't done. Asphyxiation. You drugged up to the eyeballs so you

pass out and have no idea what I'm doing to you. A couple of examples, just to let you know what I'm after."

This had turned sinister quickly. She wasn't sure what to do or say. A 'no' would get her into trouble, but she wasn't into any really *kinky shit. Dangerous shit.*

"That's a bit...too far for me," she said. "A grand wouldn't be enough." She hoped that last bit put him off pursuing this.

"Then I'll pay you more—it'll buy your silence."

Shit. He isn't going to give up.

And by mentioning silence, he didn't want anyone knowing the sort of thing that got him off. Fair enough, she doubted anyone *would just throw it out there that they had a penchant for extra-weird stuff in the bedroom, and if people found out, they'd think he was well odd, but this was too much, and he was frightening her now.*

"You don't need to pay me to keep quiet," she said. "I'm well aware of the rules."

"Just checking. So, how much more, Honey, to let me put a plastic bag over your head until you pass out?"

He was being serious. Shit. Shit!

"Um, a grand on top of the grand already paid for sex."

"And what about the drugs?"

"Another grand."

What the fuck was she doing, basically signing up for this? The money wasn't the allure now, keeping herself safe was—safer than the scenario involving a plastic bag and drugs; he'd already told her, if she talked about him, he'd be angry. He could be a nasty piece of work when he wanted to, and she wasn't indispensable, he'd discard her and look for someone else if she didn't meet his expectations.

"I don't like the idea of you doing whatever you want, though, me not knowing about it."

"It doesn't matter what you like the idea of, you know that."

His eyes seemed to glint with something evil, as if he'd been possessed. That was stupid, demons didn't exist, but dark passengers did. People carried those around with them all the time. He definitely had one, but he was clever at hiding it in front of her. Until tonight, and apart from his warnings about her keeping their affair secret, he'd acted fine, as if he was normal. Was it like Valerie had said? Had the softly-softly come to an end now?

"What…what would you do to me? When I was…out of it?"

"That's the beauty of it. You'd never know. And what you don't know can't hurt you. That's the saying, isn't it?"

He took another two envelopes out. They hadn't been in the glove box, so he must have had them on him the whole time. He'd planned this, and somehow, he'd known how much money she'd ask for. Was she that transparent? That easy to control?

He placed them on the table. "Your choice whether you pick those up or not, but we both know you will. After all, if you don't…"

He was wrong, she didn't have a choice. Or she did, but if she refused to put that money in her bag, she'd pay for it in some way. He might get nasty and beat her up. Might even kill her. He'd laid down the ground rules from day one, and she'd agreed to them, heady with the idea of belonging to him for a while, being his sole bit on the side. Chosen. Never, though, had she suspected this offer would have been dished out. A plastic bag. Drugs.

He'd lured her into a false sense of security, she could see that now. She'd thought she was the one who'd changed him because he'd treated her well with all those shows and fancy dinners. She'd convinced *herself she was special, the only one in a long line of women he'd found an affinity with.*

How could she have been so stupid? Hadn't he said he manipulated until he got what he wanted? That he could talk the hind legs off a donkey when persuading people to bend to his will? That no matter what, no one ever said no, and that was why his business was so successful?

She was going to have to go through with this. "What if it goes wrong and I die?"

He shrugged. "So what?"

Oh. Oh, she'd told herself he didn't care for her, love her, that he never would, but it still burned to hear that he didn't give a shit if she snuffed it. That her death could be passed off as some erotic game, one she'd indulged in by herself. There had been a news article about it not so long ago, a man found dead with a bag over his head, a noose around his neck, a sex game gone wrong. Was that where he'd got the idea from? It had been a big story, so he was bound to have heard about it. People had dined out on it for days in the local.

Her dying. Was this his way of getting rid of her for good? Ensuring her silence despite her promises of keeping quiet? Where would he put her body? Would she be discarded like rubbish? Or left in this hotel, in a room, for the maid to find in the morning?

And what had she done for him to go in this direction? She scoured her mind for a snippet that would tell her when she'd messed up. Oh God. Had he followed her? Seen her going to Valerie's? Did he know she'd told her about him? Had her sister blabbed to someone, and he'd found out?

No, Valerie had promised to keep it quiet. She didn't want Bear in the know.

"I don't plan on you dying, though." He smiled.

She relaxed, although the idea of passing out and him doing whatever he wanted to her held no appeal.

Regardless, she picked up the money and placed it in her bag.

Yvette woke, glancing around. This wasn't the hotel room they'd gone to after dinner. Before she'd passed out, the plastic bag hadn't made an appearance, so he must have gone down the drug route and put it over her head while she slept. She recalled drinking wine, wine he'd poured with his back to her, and as her head was muzzy now, he'd clearly given her a hefty dose of something.

This had the strains of a serial killer about it. Wasn't that what they did? Slipped something into *drinks? Only he'd been open about it beforehand, had, to all intents and purposes, got permission from her before he'd acted it out. What was next, though? Her death? Would he play with her for a few more 'sessions' as he'd put it, then get rid of her for good?*

She blinked at the sight of metal beer barrels, clear tubes coming out of them, the lager and beer turning them shades of yellow, amber, and brown. Weird clicks echoed, and she assumed someone was pulling a pint upstairs. It was obvious she was in a pub, but which one? And why was she here and not at the hotel?

She imagined him carrying her out over his shoulder. Had someone stopped him to ask what he was doing? Had he fobbed them off, saying she was drunk and he was taking her home? Or had he gone out the back way like some deviant?

She checked her body. Still dressed. Still had her shoes on. Her handbag sat beside her, and she snatched it up, drawing the zip across to check if the envelopes were there.

They were.

So she hadn't dreamt this whole, bizarre thing.

Aching from having slept on the concrete floor, she pushed herself to her feet and slung her bag strap over her shoulder. Wobbled a bit. Steadied herself by placing her palm to the brick wall. A set of double doors, made of planks, let in daylight where the wood didn't quite meet, and she headed there. A padlock kept them secure, a key dangling from it, and she twisted it. Took the lock off and opened one of the doors to peer out into a yard. More beer barrels — empty, she suspected — and plastic crates stacked with used brown, green, and transparent bottles.

The gate ahead drew her, and she went out into a backstreet. She looked up and down it, a stretch of grass at one end, a path leading God knew where at the other. She turned to check the back of the buildings to get some idea of where she was. A sign for a chemist told her she was in a shopping area, so she walked towards the grass and turned right, going past the side of a building. She came out in an unfamiliar place, her nerves on edge, her knees almost going out from under her. What drug had he given her? She felt sick, weak, as if she had the flu.

All but staggering along, she ignored the shoppers giving her curious or disgusted glances — did she look a mess, doing the obvious walk of shame? — and found a bus stop. Stared at the listed route. She was in the East End, though exactly where, she had no clue.

She waited for the bus to arrive and got on, paying to get to the main terminal where she'd take another bus home. Was dumping her in that cellar all part of the fantasy? Was *he leaning towards being a serial killer and she'd been a dry run? Would he expect her to tell him how she'd felt when she'd woken up and he'd get off on it?*

She'd known who he was from the start, had thought she'd had his measure, but she hadn't. This was beyond normal, so much so, she was convinced he had a second dark side, one nobody knew about.

Nobody except the women he played games with.

Chapter Eight

George had been ignoring Janet's calls. He contemplated blocking her. What did she want? Another go at changing him? To ask if they could try again? No, he didn't think she'd go down that road. She wouldn't want to get egg on her face when he told her the end meant the end, no going back.

A text bleep sounded, and he sighed, accessing his messages. She was a persistent cow, he'd give her that. He couldn't think of what could be so important that she'd have to follow up three missed calls with a message, though.

Rip the plaster off. Get it over and done with.

He opened the text.

JANET: URGENT! NEED YOUR HELP WITH A CLIENT. WE DON'T HAVE TO MEET UP, BUT I'D RATHER SAY WHAT IT IS THAN WRITE IT DOWN, SO CAN YOU PICK UP WHEN I RING YOU, PLEASE?

He wasn't sure if she was being bossy or stating a polite request. Bristling nonetheless, he stabbed her name in his contact list and went into his bedroom to take the call while Greg nursed his jaw downstairs. He'd had a back tooth pulled and wasn't in the best of moods.

She answered straight away.

"Janet," George said, brusque, but there was no point in being sentimental.

"Hi."

A weird pause ensued, where she possibly didn't know what to say, maybe:

How are you? All right.

Have you been okay? Yep.

Do you miss me? Nope.

Maddened by the silence, he snapped, "What's the problem?"

She tutted. "No need to bite my head off. God. This call is for *your* benefit, so don't get stroppy with me."

"My benefit?" He couldn't think what she could tell him that he'd need to know. "Out with it then, I haven't got all day."

"Do you know what? Forget it. You can find out by yourself, if you ever do. People have been laughing behind your back for a long time, and if you don't want to know who they are and what one of them has done, fuck you."

The line went dead.

He blinked a few times, shocked by her vehemence but intrigued more than he cared to admit. He dialled her again.

She answered with a terse, "What?"

"I'm sorry. I'm in the middle of something, and I'm in a shitty mood."

"I can tell. Are you prepared to be polite now?"

"Yep."

"Good. I've got a new client. She started last week. She's just phoned me from her car, saying something about her sister killing a child. I've checked the local news. It's true—and it

107

happened on *your* estate. I'm surprised Janine hasn't got hold of you yet to help her find the killer."

The mention of a child's death incensed him. "She's likely too busy." He cursed the fact that *they'd* been busy today, plus none of their men on the streets had thought a kid being killed warranted him and Greg being told. *They'd know it wasn't us, so maybe that's why.*

"Hmm." Janet tapped something. Probably her long nails on her desk. "My client is probably on your shit list so you'll be aware of her, but from speaking to her, I've gathered she wants to get away from her sister and the business they run. Whatever her sister's done, my client wants no part of it."

"Stop beating around the bush. Who is it?"

"Sienna." She paused. "Weggley. And before you go off on one, she really doesn't want to be associated with Hannah anymore, and based on what she's done to that little girl, I can't say I blame her."

"What happened to the kid?"

"She was shot."

"Jesus. I've not long seen the pair of them. Well, this morning." He checked his watch. Two-fifteen p.m. Anger, bright and hot, sprang to life in his veins, and he wasn't sure if it was Mad George or Ruffian knocking at his mental door to be let in. *A nipper. What a fucking bitch.* "I shot Hannah's finger off, actually."

"Fucking hell. If I tell you where Sienna is, will you speak to her calmly? She's easily fixed if she's treated the right way, and I don't want you ballsing anything up."

George remembered what Greg had said about Janet, how she'd been using George as a project. "Ah, you've got a new pet."

"Excuse me?"

"Doesn't matter. How do I know this isn't a ruse? They could be setting me up."

"Hannah's having an operation at the moment and won't be going home until tomorrow. This is Sienna's only window of opportunity to speak to you. I could tell you about her childhood, what I know of it so far, but that would be unethical. Believe me, she needs our help. She's been forced to work in the loan shark business since she was young."

He thought back to how Sienna had behaved earlier at the house. True, she hadn't stuck up for her sister, which was odd, considering George

109

would batter anyone senseless if they shot Greg, and she'd moved away from Finnegan after he'd been shot as if to distance herself from the situation.

He sighed. "Okay, but Greg won't be pleased about having to go out. He's been to the dentist."

"Right, well, not my problem. She's at The Angel."

"Phone her back and tell her to knock on the parlour door and get Amaryllis to let her in."

"I'm not one of your minions, George, so don't speak to me like that, dishing out orders."

"Do you want my fucking help or not?"

"I do."

"Then shut up."

He cut the call, and the irritation Janet had inspired in him during the last few weeks of their relationship reared its narked head again. He knocked it back into the box he'd stuffed it into after she'd ended things, not wanting to deal with it. Taking a different gun from the safe and putting the one he'd used on Hannah and Finnegan inside, ready to be disposed of later, he went downstairs, preparing himself to break the news to Greg.

George stood at the living room doorway. "Sorry, bruv, but we've got a job to do."

"Bloody hell…" It had come out like 'ruddy ow'; his mouth likely felt massive after the anaesthetic.

"Err, best you don't speak. I'll do all the talking when we get there. Oh, and on the way, I need to let you in on a few things."

"Like what?"

"I've been busy this morning."

"Zesus rist."

George smiled. "Come on. I'll even ask Amaryllis to put a straw in your cuppa if you be a good boy."

Greg pushed off the sofa and brushed past him, stomping to the kitchen then into the adjoining garage. George followed, and they got into the BMW, seeing as it was official business.

George coasted down their street. "It's like this…" He went on to tell him about his exploits last night and those from earlier.

"But we agreed to wait another three months before we picked Pete up," Greg muffled out.

"I just about understood that garbled nonsense." George continued with his little story, why he'd helped Genevieve, how come he'd ended up at the Weggleys' 'office', and most of what had happened there.

Greg groaned. "You thot her in the 'and?"

"Yeah, she dogged me off. Then I shot some bloke in the head before he shot me."

Greg leant his head back and closed his eyes.

George grimaced. "But get this. Hannah killed a kid last night. A little girl. Look it up on the internet for me so we know what's what there."

Greg sighed and took their joint work phone from the cup holder.

"Sienna needs our help, seeing as her sister's lost the plot." George anticipated Greg moaning so went with, "Yeah, I know, she doesn't deserve it after running that business behind our backs, but Janet says she's been wanting out, so now's her chance. She could help us get our hands on Hannah."

Greg stared at the screen. "I'll read the beginning of the article. *Eight-year-old Libby Nivens was shot last night in her own home. Two people had come to the house, asking to see her father. When she wouldn't open the door, they shot her through it.*"

"Fuck me, poor little sod. Where were the parents?"

"It doesn't say."

George swung the car into the driveway down the side of The Angel and parked round the back. To occupy his mind, taking it away from Libby, he checked his gun had enough bullets in case Sienna had arranged an ambush, then got out of the car. Greg followed him to the security door of the parlour, and George stabbed the code into the keypad. He entered, Amaryllis smiling from behind the reception desk opposite.

"Afternoon, you two," she said. "She's in Debbie's old room. Do you want a cuppa?"

George nodded. "Greg needs a straw."

"Kuck off."

George smirked and walked in there. Sienna looked different to earlier. She'd had her hair, nails, and makeup done, but she still had her grungy clothes on. She stared at him, fear in her eyes, and darted her attention to Greg who stomped in and flopped down on a nearby sofa. Why had she had a makeover? Was it a disguise? If she thought they were going to hide her in one of their safe houses, she had another think coming. To make up for her part in running the loan shark business behind their backs, she could earn their forgiveness by playing a part in capturing Hannah.

George closed the door and locked it. "Fancy seeing you twice in one day," he said in his Scottish accent.

Greg snorted.

Sienna gawped.

"Shut your trap or you'll catch flies," George said. "Yeah, it was me at your gaff earlier." He leant on the door, one hand on his gun at his waistband so she was aware he'd use it if he had to. "Janet got hold of me. So come on, give us a bit of background info so I can decide if we should feel sorry for you or not."

"You won't shoot me, will you?"

"Depends whether you had anything to do with that murder last night."

"I only found out about it today. As soon as I knew, I left one of our blokes to torch the loan house and came straight here."

"What bloke?"

"I'd rather not say."

"Look, I admire your loyalty an' all that, but I need to see if we're on the same page. What. Bloke?"

She huffed out a breath. "Two-Time."

"Right. Spout your crap, then. I haven't got all day."

By the time she'd finished, he *did* feel sorry for her. He spotted himself in her, or maybe he spotted Greg, the more rational of the siblings, whereas Hannah sounded like she had her own Ruffian thing going on, except she couldn't control it.

Sienna's upbringing had been a hard one, and she wasn't even Hannah's sister, although she didn't know why. Some bloke, an uncle type, had let it slip. The shit she'd been through, and those scars on her stomach... Some must date back years they looked that old, but it hadn't only been Hannah who'd cut her.

"By all accounts, you're good at what you do," George said. "I've been asking around, finding out who I'm dealing with before I made my move. You're the more...stable one, the one willing to listen to reason when clients can't pay up, so for that, we're willing to help you. I agree, Hannah needs stopping. I'd have maybe kneecapped her next if she hadn't killed that kid, but as it stands, she needs torturing, sorting, and you're going to help me bring her down."

"What do I have to do?"

No hesitation. Not an ounce of slyness in her expression.

George cocked his head. "I don't have to ask why you want to disassociate yourself from her, but what's your endgame? What do you actually want?"

"Freedom. To make my own choices. To find out who the hell my real parents are. To run my own business."

"You can't do that on our patch without permission."

"I know."

"How do you feel about working for us? Running a loan company in our name."

"I'd still be under someone's thumb, though. The whole point is for me to not have to answer to anyone."

George shrugged. "Fair enough, go it alone, but if you plan to do it on Cardigan, you'll need to pay us protection money, it's as simple as that."

"Fine by me."

"That's that sorted, then. Now, Janet said Hannah's out of commission until tomorrow, which suits us because we've got time to plan. What will she do when she finds out the house has been torched?"

"Dunno. I'm not telling her it was Two-Time."

"Best you don't, because as of this morning, he works for us."

"I had a feeling. Him picking up the casings and bullets kind of tipped me off."

"What are you on about?"

"He did it before he torched the place. Probably so the bullets couldn't be traced back to you."

"They can't anyway, but it's good to know he's doing what he's paid for."

"So he was going to be your inside man, was he?"

"Hmm. Only now you'll join him—until Hannah's dead, obviously." He finally sat, taking his gun out and, keeping it in hand, rested it on his knee. "Is she the type to stay at home tomorrow, recuperate?"

"No, she'll want to find new premises, get the word out where we're based. People are due to pay money back today, and with nowhere to go to drop it off, she'll need to get something up and running quick."

"Right, you'll just happen to have found somewhere today. She'll think you've done it for her benefit, what with her having a poorly hand."

"She'll have a go at me for doing it without asking."

"So? Once she sees it, she'll be all right."

"Got something in mind, have you?"

"Yeah." He smiled. You want her dead, yes?"

Sienna nodded.

"Then there's one only question left that you need to answer. Are you killing her or am I?"

Chapter Nine

Yvette had missed a period. She thought back to that time, when he'd asked her to play at being an escort. They never used condoms, he didn't like them, but she was on the pill so hadn't been that bothered. When she'd finally got home that horrible morning, she'd showered and gone straight to bed, seeing as it had been a Saturday. The drugs must have been strong, because she hadn't woken until eleven *that night and, after a quick meal of beans on toast, she'd returned to bed, sleeping until nine a.m. She usually took her pill in the morning and hadn't remembered to do it. She'd been too disturbed and frightened, not to mention tired, to think of anything but forgetting what he must have done to her while she'd been out of it.*

What was she going to do? She didn't want a baby but couldn't stand the idea of having an abortion. And how the hell would she tell him? Maybe he wouldn't need to know. She wouldn't show for a good while yet, and he'd ditch her by the time she got a bump.

This had been swirling inside her head for two weeks now. What if the drugs harmed the baby? It could be born deformed and all sorts.

The bell jangled to signal the end of work, and she left the building, praying he wouldn't be outside, his beard and wig hiding who he was from anyone watching. But he was *there, on the other side of the road, leaning on a lamppost, hands in the pockets of his grey suit trousers, the toe of one shoe pointed to the path. She smiled, as she always did, although today it was a strain not to grimace. She wanted out, needed him to leave her alone, couldn't risk doing another drug fantasy. If she told him she was pregnant, it would all be over, so why was she hesitant?*

He got in yet another of his cars and waited. She walked across the road, climbed in, and left her seat belt off. These meetings didn't usually include him driving her home, driving her anywhere, they were to arrange another date. He didn't trust using his phone, nor would he pop a note through her front door.

"Did you enjoy yourself last time?" He laughed, slapping the steering wheel. "Oh, I forgot, you don't know what happened for the second half of it."

She laughed, too. It was what he'd expect. "What did you get up to?"

She had an idea. Bruises on her rib area and the tops of her arms had given a good indication, as had the red marks around her neck. He'd hit her, the rib bruises in the shape of fists, the ones on her arms fingerprints, and her throat, well, that was obvious. She'd had to wear a chiffon scarf for days.

"I played out teaching you a lesson," he said. "You know, what would happen if you ever disobeyed the rules. Was your neck sore?"

"A little."

"Then I didn't squeeze hard enough. Next time, I will."

Next time... This had to stop. It was insanity to keep seeing him. He was more dangerous than he'd ever let on. Who the fuck thought it was okay to do this shit?

"I'm pregnant," she blurted and stared ahead through the windscreen, her heart hammering, because she'd crossed the line now, there was no going back.

"You what?"

"I forgot to take my tablet… I was groggy, the drugs…"

"That's no excuse. Why didn't you take the morning after pill?"

"Like I said, I was groggy and—"

The elbow to her chest winded her, and she struggled to breathe. He twisted round and gripped her throat, and she shuddered at having to feel it, to experience it tightening, choking her.

"You stupid fucking cow. What did you think would happen, that I'd marry you? Who are you, one of those people who get up the duff to snag a rich man? A gold digger, is that what you are? Well, let's get one thing straight, that kid, if you're even pregnant, isn't mine. It might well be, but to everyone else, no, it's nothing to do with me."

Blackness crowded the edges of her vision, and she raised her hands to clamp them to his wrist. She tugged, but it didn't do anything except incite him to dig his fingertips harder. Desperate for someone to help *her, she stared at workers leaving the building, their heads down, too intent on getting home to care about what was going on in the car. All they wanted was their dinner, yet she wanted air, such a simple yet important thing that was running out by the second. She tugged some more, and her body arched by itself, her feet drumming on the footwell. Then he let her go, throwing himself back into his seat and starting the engine.*

"People like you...fucking hell."

He drove off. She panted and wheezed, contemplating opening the door and flinging herself out onto the road, anything to get away from him. Where was he taking her? What would he do when they got there?

"Please, I'll get rid of it, I swear."

"You'd fucking better. I can't stand to breathe the same air as you. Fucking traitorous bitch."

He swerved and parked at the kerb, other cars whipping by, and leant over, opened her door, and shoved her. She fell out, her side banging on the verge, the lower half of her legs still in the car. Quickly, she snatched her feet out and scrabbled backwards, dried grass stubble poking into her palms. She stared at him, his eyes flashing with that dark passenger she'd seen before.

"This is over," he said. "You're a liability. If I find out you've opened your mouth… Get rid of that thing inside you, or I'll come for you when you least expect it, and I won't let go of your throat next time."

He drove off, the passenger door snapping shut with the force of his speed, and the car disappeared around a bend. Was that it? A quick strangle, a warning, and he was gone? No taking her to an abortion clinic? He'd discarded her just like that, thinking his word was enough, that she'd obey him. She would, but wasn't he taking a big risk?

Another vehicle stopped, and a woman got out, coming towards her, hands up to show she meant no harm. "Are you okay?"

Fuck, Yvette recognised her from work. Delia. "Um, just had a row with my boyfriend, and he kicked me out of the car."

"Jesus, and he's still your boyfriend?" Delia peered up the road, probably checking if his car reappeared.

"Not bloody likely." Yvette sensed a bruise forming where she'd hit the verge. Would the jolt on the ground have hurt the baby? Would she lose it? He'd love it if that happened, and maybe she wouldn't mind…it would take things out of her hands. A miscarriage would be his fault, and she'd have her conscience eased.

Was she wicked for thinking that? Or just human?

Delia crouched. "Do you need a lift?"

Could Yvette risk involving her? Yes, it was only a lift, but what if he'd parked up somewhere, got out, and currently watched them? But walking didn't appeal, so selfishly, she said, "If you wouldn't mind."

Delia helped her up. "Of course I don't mind, I wouldn't have offered if I did, would I. Are you going to report him to the police? People like him need locking up."

"People like him always get away with it. I'm okay, it's fine. Or it will be now he's dumped me."

On the drive to Yvette's, Delia chattered on. "I've just got out of a bad relationship and don't have a nice word to say about the male species at the moment. Arseholes, the lot of them. Steer clear, that's my advice. Even if he comes sniffing round saying sorry, it's a lie. Those types always do that, and before you know it, you're taking him back, then the cycle starts all over again. It isn't worth it, believe me."

Yvette agreed. She wouldn't have the guts to touch another man for a long time to come, not even with a bargepole.

"You're what?" Valerie glanced around at the others in the coffee shop during their usual weekly meet-up. "Say it a bit louder, why don't you, so the whole place can hear. Fucking hell, what were you thinking?"

"I wasn't. I just wanted to go to bed when I got home. I didn't feel well, and taking my pill was the last thing on my mind." Should she tell her? Reveal the bizarre secret, the games they'd played, the way he'd used her to be whoever his fantasy wanted? "He…"

"He what?"

Yvette took a deep breath. "He's nuts in the head. On the last date, he drugged me. I passed out, and he shagged me."

"He shagged you while you **slept**?" Valerie stared at her, hard. "That is beyond dodgy. Jesus Christ, who the fuck does he think he is? Are you okay?"

"Hmm."

"So what happened after that?"

"He left me in the cellar of a pub."

Valerie widened her eyes, a red flush creeping up her neck and into her cheeks. "Eh? That doesn't make sense. Why even do that? Why not just take you home? And what bloody pub was it?"

"I don't know, I didn't exactly feel up to finding out." Yvette skipped the sordid details, giving just enough so her sister got the general idea.

"No wonder he was seeing you, because you can bet other women wouldn't do that sort of shit."

"Are you saying I'm loose or something? Up for anything?"

"I didn't mean it like that. You're easily led, eager to please, always have been. I worried he was taking advantage, and I was right. I won't ask why you agreed for him to drug you, but… He left you in a strange cellar, kicked you out of his car… You'd better have that abortion, because if he finds out you've kept it, there'll be hell to pay."

"I'm not getting rid of it."

"Yvette! You have to. You're free of him now, so why invite trouble? What if he puts on another disguise, follows you around in one of the cars he's been using, and he sees your bump?"

"He won't bother. I'm nothing to him now, I've been thrown away. Why would he even think about me again, enough to follow me? No, someone else will have taken my place already, you'll see."

"No, I won't see, because he doesn't openly have women, does he. I can see now how he gets his jollies without people knowing, threatening women to keep quiet." Valerie sighed. "Well, at least this is one secret I can chuck away now. I hated keeping it from Bear that you were seeing him."

"Is that all you've got out of this, relief? Thanks a fucking lot." Yvette folded her arms. While she understood Valerie's reaction, it still hurt. The one thing her sister had focused on out of all that was she didn't have to worry anymore. The fact Yvette had been drugged, abused, strangled in that car, thrown out, that was now by the bloody by. Fucking hell!

"You have to look on the bright side." Valerie sipped her coffee.

"Then my bright side is that I'll have a little baby to care for soon. At least then I'll have someone else to think about other than myself. I didn't like seeing that side of me, where I was willing to do anything just to get a few free meals Up West. It was disgusting."

"Stop it. You can't keep it."

"Why not? I'll work until my bump's too noticeable. I'll get maternity pay, go back to work when it's a couple of months old."

"And how will you manage on maternity pay? How will you find the money for a childminder, because I'm not looking after it."

"I'll cross that bridge when I come to it."

"Do you have any idea how much kids cost? Hannah needs something new every five minutes because she's growing so fast. Then there's the school trips, all that. It's one thing after another. I can afford it, but can you?"

"That's it, rub it in that you're swimming in money. You know damn well I can't shell out much."

"Then don't have a baby, it's as simple as that."

Yvette saw the sense in what her sister had said, but... "I'll manage. Go on the dole or something until it goes to school."

"Are you being serious?"

"Why not? Loads of other people do it."

Valerie stared outside at shoppers going about their business. She sighed. "The benefit system isn't there so you can choose to go on it because it's convenient."

"I know, but it's an avenue I can use."

"Look, if you insist on going ahead, I'll buy all the gear, the pram and whatnot, but after that, it's your problem."

The gesture brought tears to Yvette's eyes. "I could give up the house, switch it for a flat like the council said. He won't know where I live, then."

"That's one option, but make sure they know you've got a bun in the oven so they don't put you in some poky one-bedroom effort."

It could work, couldn't it?

Yvette would have to make sure it did, because despite not wanting a baby yet, it was inside her, and she wasn't giving it up for anyone.

Chapter Ten

Janine Sheldon couldn't tear her gaze away from the little body on the slab. As a DI, she was used to attending post-mortems, although she usually shied away from them and someone else did it in her place. This one, though... She needed the anger of seeing such a small person laid out like this to fuel her in finding the killer. She had to get justice for eight-year-old Libby Nivens, someone who should have been leaving school around now, eager to get home and watch Disney films. Instead, here she was, the life shot out of her, no more *Cinderella*, her favourite, according to her mother.

Janine's new DS, Colin Broadly, stood by the door in his protectives as if ready to bolt. An older man, he was jaded by everything he'd seen in the force and just wanted to bide his time until retirement, doing the minimum. His attitude suited Janine perfectly, and she had five years of his company before he toddled off to tend to an allotment or whatever the hell he planned to do once he left the job.

Her prayers had been answered — her previous DS, a nosy little shite, had moved on to the NCA after she'd encouraged him to go into a field where his inquisitiveness would be put to better use. He'd been suspicious of Janine, always asking questions, and she'd had to get him off her team before he poked into things too much when she was covering up for The Brothers. From what she'd gleaned so far, Colin wouldn't give a toss *what* she was up to so long as he didn't have to do any work.

"All right there, Colin?" she asked.

"Err, yeah." He hugged himself.

"It's going to be a tough one." Janine glanced at Jim, the pathologist. "How the hell do you cope when they're so young?"

"Not very well, to be honest, although I put on a brave front." Jim leant over and inspected the bullet wounds: one on the face, one near the heart, and the other in the stomach. "The trajectory of this one"—he indicated the stomach—"shows a deliberate angle to the gun. For the belly to have been hit, given her height and where the bottom of the glass panels in the door were, if the bullet had been fired straight, which would be a normal thing to do if you wanted to shoot someone, it would have entered her chest. For whatever reason, the killer perhaps *wanted* to hit the stomach. Based on which site would have killed her, I'm saying, and will probably discover I'm right, that the bullets entered her in this order: stomach, chest, face."

"So you think the stomach is important?"

"Yes, as I believe it was the first shot, so a conscious decision to wound her there. If you want someone dead quickly, it's a straight shot to the most fatal place, you don't go for the stomach, as death from that is bleeding out, which takes a while, plus there's more chance the victim could be saved. You want the job done and dusted so you can get out of there, so the heart or head would be the first choice for an immediate kill. Of course, I could be talking out of my backside, wanting the stomach to be important so you've got something to go on. I'm desperate for you to find whoever did this to her."

"Because it's a child?"

"I want justice for all my patients, but a kid? Yes. What the hell happened last night for this to be the result?"

"A witness, Mr Danes, saw someone ring the bell. He'd been on his way home from work, the late shift. Someone in black—he thinks it was either a slim, short man or a woman—asked to speak to Libby's father; they spoke through the letterbox. It seems Libby wouldn't open the door because the killer said, 'Open it, you little bitch, or I'll shoot you.' Someone was with the offender, tall, wide, and both had balaclavas on. Clearly, Libby didn't do what they wanted. Mr Danes saw a gun being raised and hid behind a parked Transit to phone the police, but he changed his mind, too scared in case they heard him speaking and turned the gun on him."

"Understandable. Can you imagine being in that situation? You'd know damn well whether you phoned the police at that point or not, someone was going to be murdered."

"Hmm. He's going to feel guilty no matter what. So, shots were fired, and they got into a dark car and drove off. Mr Danes then called it in."

"Was she alone in the house?"

"No. Her dad was asleep on the sofa, the mother at work. Libby had been told never to answer the door without checking with her parents first. The father woke when he heard the gunshots."

"To find his daughter dead. Tragic." Jim used a monocle to study Libby's face. "Multiple glass fragments embedded in the skin, peppered throughout her hair. Tiny, some powder-like."

"The lead SOCO said only three casings were found, so the killer could likely see Libby's shape through the mottled-glass door panels—they knew exactly where to shoot, they *knew* it was a child and didn't care."

"All bullets are still in the body," Jim said. "No exit wounds. From what we can see here, she was a healthy child, well cared for. This one's going to haunt me in my sleep. I mean, look at her. Innocent. Only following rules set by her parents."

"I know. Bloody awful."

"Any leads on the car?" Jim appeared hopeful, his eyes above the mask wide.

"No. They avoided cameras, which tells me they're local."

Jim sighed. "Okay, I'm going to open her up. Are you staying?"

Janine nodded. "For once."

Jim smiled sadly. "I understand why. It *does* seem worse when it's a child, doesn't it."

Janine ended up walking out after the first incision. It was too much, seemed too brutal to cut someone so young. She'd left Colin there, stating she'd catch up with him later as she had a few people she wanted to speak to, neighbours and the like, even though uniforms had already covered that last night. In reality, she needed the time to speak to the twins. If they hadn't heard about Libby's death she'd be surprised—and if they had, why hadn't they contacted her? They'd be gunning for whoever had murdered that little girl, unless they were doing it under the radar and were too busy to get hold of her at the moment.

In the car, she drove off until she found a lay-by and used her burner to ring George and Greg.

"I wondered if you'd pipe up eventually," George said.

"I'm shocked you haven't got hold of me."

"We've not long found out about the kid. Fucking disgusting. We were busy this morning so didn't check the news. Any leads on who did it?"

"No."

"Good job we already know, then, isn't it."

"How the *fuck* do you find these things out so fast? I'm the copper here, not you two."

"Friends in the right places, people willing to talk. You know what it's like. Most folks around here don't want to speak to the police."

"Who did it?"

"Some woman I shot earlier. She's minus a finger. Mind you, I didn't know she was the killer at the time, I shot her for another reason. We found out about the murder via Janet."

"How the hell did *she* know?"

"One of her clients is related to the killer."

"So we're going to discuss this using 'the killer' as a name because you're dealing with it?"

"Yeah. Got something set up for tomorrow. The killer just so happens to be having an operation on her finger stump. As for the person who was likely an accomplice last night, he's with her. Loyal to her. She probably ordered him to stay with her the whole time."

"She sounds like she's heavily into crime, someone like you, if she can order grown men about."

"She's not been anyone we were too concerned about but lately has got worse."

"Is she on the database? At least tell me that."

"Probably."

"I can always ring round the hospitals, you know, find out who's been admitted with a gunshot wound."

"Good luck, because she isn't in one."

Janine thumped the steering wheel. "Where is she, then?"

"Some clinic. Listen, it's best we sort it because it's linked to something we're already dealing with. Long story, won't bore you."

"So you're saying you're going to get rid of her, and that poor family are going to live the rest of their lives not knowing what happened to the killer? No justice for their daughter?"

George sniffed. "I'll make an exception. I can drop the bodies off and let you know where they are—we plan to get hold of the accomplice as well. I'll make sure to get the gun she used."

"That's something, then. So I need to tread water in the meantime, I take it."

"The usual drill."

She loved earning the extra money from the twins, but at times like this, when she had to deliberately stall investigations, it tired her out. She was always on edge, worrying her DCI would action something which could lead to whoever had committed the crime. He left her alone for the most part, but with something like this, when it involved a kiddie, she wasn't sure he'd sit back and keep out of it.

"I'll try my best, but because of who the victim is, my boss might—"

"Try harder than your best."

He cut the call, and she leant her head back and closed her eyes, hating the way he did that. She owed George, he'd killed another officer for her during the refugee case in the spring, but it still grated on her that he dictated how things went.

DI Keith Sykes' death had been put down to a sex trafficking organisation called The Network, an execution she was more than happy to let someone else take the blame for. Many Network employees had been found and awaited trial for various offences, but the big boss, Teo de Luca, was in the wind. Tipped off, most likely, and at one point she'd wondered if that name was an alias, but a dig into the records, with the help of the Italian police, had debunked that theory. He was real, and while there was a financial trail in what he spent his money on, no property or cars were in his name. It seemed he'd rented a house from the owner, who was also AWOL, and Janine suspected they were one and the same, as the homeowner couldn't be found either, so de Luca must have a third name he'd used to escape to God knew where.

The investigation into finding him was still ongoing. She'd worked on it with the DCI, and when the leads had gone cold, it had been passed to another team. Somewhere out there, de Luca continued his sordid business, she was sure of it, but she couldn't torment herself about him slipping through the net when crimes continued to happen on her patch and victims needed her full attention.

Like Libby.

She switched the engine on and drove off, wondering what sort of woman was willing to shoot a child. *Why* had she needed to speak to Libby's father? He'd seemed to have no idea, but it didn't take a calculator to add up that he must have been into something dodgy for a killer to come calling. Last night, when she'd questioned him, he'd been willing to hide the identity of who it might be, even though his child was dead. What could be so bad that he'd withhold information? Did he need to keep something from his wife? Was he bothered about any recriminations from her when his main focus should be helping the police catch the murderer?

What could he have done that was so awful?

Maybe he feels so guilty about her death, that it's his fault, he can't face it at the moment.

She should speak to him again now he'd got over the initial shock. Make a show of at least *trying* to find out what had gone on. Her DCI would think it was weird if she didn't, and he was the last person she needed poking into this case.

She sighed and parked outside the cordon at the crime scene. The parents were staying three doors down with family. A quick text to Colin, letting him know where she was, and she got out of the car, willing tomorrow to come quickly so she could tell her boss an anonymous call had come in about two bodies who would just happen to be the people they were looking for. Then another investigation would sprout from it: why had they been killed, and who by?

She'd have to sweep that answer firmly under the rug.

Somehow.

Chapter Eleven

Seething to the point her teeth ached from clenching them so hard, Hannah lay in her private room at the clinic, her eyes closed, Donkey's heavy breathing a comfort. He'd stayed here the whole time, loyal to the last. Which was more than could be said for Sienna. Where was she? Why hadn't she come to visit? What the hell was *wrong* with her? It had been written in stone since they were kids that Hannah was the boss of her, so why was Sienna rebelling against that lately? There was the revelation from Uncle Abel that Sienna and Hannah weren't sisters; could that be it?

They'd gone to visit him, Hannah needing to see someone who'd been with her for as far back as she could remember, a steadying influence, Sienna grumbling that now he was in a care home, he could rot for all she gave a shit. Ungrateful bitch. Especially after all he'd done for the family. They owed him, and a visit once a week wasn't too much to ask, was it?

Uncle Abel dribbled more than usual today. While it churned Hannah's stomach, she still reached out with a tissue to mop it up. That's what you did for family, you cared for them when they couldn't care for themselves. Mum and Dad, both dying from overdoses weeks apart, had drummed it into Hannah's head that no matter what, family came first. She'd honour that, even though they weren't here to enforce it.

Abel stared at Sienna, the old sneer from days gone by crinkling his mouth. "Why the fuck are you here?"

Sienna shrugged. "Because she'd have a go if I didn't come."

Hannah bristled. It seemed a slice of the knife was in order to get her back in line.

"You weren't even meant to be a part of our unit," Abel said.

"That's just rubbish," Hannah cut in, her guts going south. She didn't need Sienna knowing the truth and would lie about it until her dying day. Mum and Dad had made her promise, and she wouldn't put them in the shit if she could help it.

"It's time she knew." Abel sighed, closed his eyes.

"Knew what?" Sienna asked.

Abel gripped the wooden arms of his chair. "You're not sisters."

Sienna stared at Hannah. "What? Is this true?"

"Of course it bloody isn't." Hannah stood. "He's rambling again. It's the meds, they send him funny. Come on, we'll leave him to have a kip."

"You normally say we have to stay here for the whole hour whether he's asleep or not." Sienna remained on her seat, arms folded.

"I can change my mind, can't I?"

"Yeah, if it suits you."

"What was that?" Hannah raised her eyebrows. "You'd better not be giving me any cheek."

Sienna tutted.

They left the room, Abel snoring, Hannah so angry *because he'd blurted the family secret. If he was going to be unpredictable, she couldn't risk him talking to Sienna again. Next time, she'd come here alone.*

Out in the car park, she took a deep breath, waiting for Sienna to either ask questions or keep quiet like she'd been taught to. With nothing forthcoming, Hannah got in the car and waited for Sienna to join her.

"He's mad, you know that, right?" Hannah fired the engine up and peeled out of her spot.

"What if there's some truth to it, though? I've never felt like I belonged."

"Rubbish, that's all it is. He's probably so loony he thinks you're someone else."

"Like who?"

"I dunno, his niece or something. He's bound to have one somewhere."

"Bloody weird thing for him to say. That we're not sisters."

"Yeah, well, mental people say odd shit all the time. Doesn't mean it's true."

Sienna stared ahead, her mouth set, her eyebrows scrunched. What was she thinking? If Sienna dug hard enough, she'd uncover the truth. Thank God Mum and Dad were dead so they wouldn't get in trouble. As for

Hannah, she could make out she wasn't aware, that she'd assumed Sienna was her sister. After all, why wouldn't she? They'd been brought up together.

She wouldn't tell Sienna. She'd already stupidly confided in Two-Time and Donkey when they'd been out on a bender. Not the facts, just that they weren't related in the way Sienna thought.

She'd have to be more careful in the future. Loose lips sank ships.

It *had* been that day Sienna had changed. What Abel had said must have wormed its way into her head. Since then, she'd been getting steadily worse with the way she spoke to Hannah, being rude, refusing to do as she was told sometimes, despite the threats of being cut if she didn't behave. Sienna hated the cuts, the way she was held down, yet she was heading for another session, what with her behaviour when that Scottish bloke had come to the house this morning. Where was the support? And when Hannah had told her to check the money, she'd seen that filthy look.

"Any news about last night?" she asked Donkey, opening her eyes and staring at the ceiling.

"Nothing we need to worry about. It's gone national, though. Because it was a kid."

"Do you think I made a mistake?" She glanced at him.

"Yep, but as long as you're not caught—"

"*You're*? You were there, too. You'll get done for it as much as me. Joint enterprise. It isn't like you told me to put my gun away, is it."

"I do as I'm told, but I'm not going down for it when it was your doing. Just so we're clear."

"So you'd abandon me?" *Like Mum and Dad did by killing themselves.*

"Who wouldn't with something like this? You went a step too far. I've been thinking about it all morning, beating myself up. You're lucky I came to collect you to bring you here. I was planning to hide out. It's one thing to be a bully, to get money out of people, but is there any need to kill them? Nivens only owed you a hundred quid. He'd paid the rest back on time, but he lost his job and just needed a month or two to find another one. He agreed to pay any interest. You made a deal, so why did we even have to go there?"

"I'm sick of people taking the piss."

"That's the nature of the business."

"I thought you had my back."

"I did, but not for something like this. If it had been Nivens you shot, it'd be different, but it wasn't, was it. Her picture's everywhere. My feed's full of it. She was only eight."

"You didn't have any remorse last night."

"I did, I just didn't show it."

"First Sienna acts weird, and now you." *Am I losing my grip on them all? If Dad were alive, he'd go fucking mental.* "What happened to the pledge? How we all agreed to stick together no matter what?"

She'd introduced it once her parents had died and Abel had gone into the home, wanting to recreate the same sense of security she'd had while growing up by adding Finnegan, Donkey, and Two-Time to the family, needing the same structure so she felt strong. She fed off people being scared of her, doing whatever she asked. Without that, she tended to be a bit lost—and being lost was a no-no. Dad had said so.

Donkey stood and parted the venetian blinds to look through the window. "The pledge means fuck all when it comes to that kid. There's only so much you can expect people to do for you. If the story hadn't blown up so big, we could have weathered the storm, but what if someone clocked the number plate and reported it?"

"Get rid of the car, then."

"What good will *that* do? They'd still see it's registered in Sienna's name, then the police would come poking around. You're linked to her, remember."

"Fuck's sake, we should have got a dodgy plate, but I didn't know I was going to kill anyone last night. It just happened."

"How can it 'just happen'?"

"The crimson lens came."

"What?"

Fuck, she hadn't meant to mention that. "You wouldn't understand. I lost it, all right?"

"Then you need to sort yourself out, learn to hold back your anger."

"She reminded me of Sienna when she was little."

"So?"

"It pissed me off that she was being a goody two-shoes when I wanted her to do what *I* wanted."

"You've been getting worse lately. I mean, look, you had your finger shot off today. Doesn't that tell you something? Why did he shoot you, that's what I want to know."

"I probably wounded his ego and he didn't like it."

"And what's happening with Finnegan?"

"Sienna's dealing with it."

"Is that wise? You've said yourself she's been chatting back, doesn't seem herself."

"Are you questioning my tactics?"

Donkey sighed. "D'you know what, there's no getting through to you. Fuck this for a game of soldiers." He walked to the door. "I'm making myself scarce for a bit. I'll be back when this has all died down."

"Don't come crawling to me when you want your job back, because someone else will have filled the position by then."

"See if I care."

"I'll do an anonymous tip-off. Ring the pigs and tell them *you* killed her."

He stormed up to the bed, leaning over her, clamping a hand around her throat. "You'd better watch yourself, lady. Accidents can happen. Cars can get ploughed into. Knives can slice throats."

Shit, she'd pushed him too far. "Get your hand off me."

"You don't get to tell me what to do anymore. I've got something on you, and if you're not careful, I'll be the one giving the rozzers a tip-off. I've got the gun, remember, and you didn't wear gloves."

"You wouldn't dare."

"Try me."

He squeezed her throat, pushed down, and any minute now, her body would automatically switch to struggle mode. Her hands would come up to grip his wrist, try to pull him off her. She didn't want that to happen, she'd look weak, so she willed herself to go limp, her lungs bursting, her arms down by her sides.

He let go just as she was about to pass out.

"Fuck with me," he said, "and you'll regret it."

He left, and she stared at the closed door, shocked he'd defied her, had the gall to choke her. It was because she was in bed, wasn't it, groggy from that operation. There was no way he'd speak to her like that if they were at the loan house, no way he'd put his hands on her otherwise.

She took a moment to compose herself, refusing to acknowledge she'd been scared, that she'd thought she was about to die. She grabbed her phone from the side table, switched it on — a bit difficult with one hand bandaged — and sat up to rest the mobile on her thigh so she could type a message to Sienna.

The responses Sienna had sent earlier fuelled Hannah's temper. Who did she think she was? Sick of being disrespected, she hammered out a reply.

HANNAH: DON'T SPEAK TO ME LIKE THAT! HAVE YOU SORTED FINNEGAN YET?

No wiggling bubbles to indicate Sienna was replying. Hannah stared at her screen for ages, but no text popped up.

She imagined slicing Sienna's belly with the knife when she finally got out of here, pinning her arms with her knees, taking her frustration out on her. In fact, she'd discharge herself now. She'd already paid the bill for the op and the clinic's silence, a bitter pill to swallow since it had cost so much, but that was the price you paid when you were someone like her. She'd known about the clinic from Mum and Dad. They'd used it when they hadn't been able to take Auntie Yvette to the hospital.

Yvette. Hannah barely remembered her these days, but she'd been nice, she knew that much. If only she hadn't gone to see that horrible man, Mum forcing her to do it.

Maybe she'd still be alive, then.

Chapter Twelve

Sienna sat in the corner of the Seven Bells with Two-Time, worried out of her mind. She'd crossed the uncrossable line by going to the twins, and if Hannah found out before they got hold of her, there'd be hell to pay. Hannah had a habit of knowing when Sienna was lying, so she'd spot something was up. Sienna would have to work hard to act in her usual way. Could she do it? Pull this off?

She had to. George and Greg were relying on her, and if she reneged on her promise to them, they'd kill her. She didn't want to die. How strange, when for the majority of her life, that was all she'd prayed for. Oblivion. A permanent way out. Now, though, she wanted to live so much it hurt. To be her own person. Free.

"So the twins believed you," Two-Time said. "That's good. They believed me, too. I'd heard they can be fair. Before, I thought they just offed anyone who'd been involved in stuff they didn't like."

"Same. Seems because I was coerced, they don't think I need to be punished. How did you get away with that? You *chose* to work for Hannah."

"George approached me first thing as I was coming out of my flat. Said he'd been watching me and he knew where I worked. He offered me a good deal if I switched sides. I lied and said she'd told me she paid them protection money, that she was working on Cardigan legitimately. It's not like he can prove it, is it? Her word against mine. I was meant to be his mole, report back to him with evidence, pictures and whatnot, but that's all changed now."

"When did she tell you she wasn't my sister?"

"We got rat-arsed one night, and she blurted it out."

"Why didn't you tell me?"

"She told me not to."

"Can't say I blame you. We've all been under threat of her hurting us. We've all done as she asked."

"She should never have cut you."

"She should never have done many things but she did." Sienna shrugged, tired from telling the twins her story. She'd covered the main points, but there was so much more they didn't know. "I can see why, though. Not saying I feel sorry for her or anything, because she could have changed once Mum and Dad died, it's just...she'd been controlled by them, moulded into a little soldier."

"Yeah, but you have to be a certain kind of person in the first place to want to do what she did to you, what she's done to some customers. Look at old Robertson. Don't try and justify her behaviour. It's wrong. Moulded or not, she should know right from wrong. You do. I do. We just needed the courage to stand up and say we weren't doing it anymore."

"It's hard. All this. I can't explain it, but I've known her as my sister all my life. She's sliced my belly, threatened me, scared me, so why do I feel guilty for setting her up?" She lowered her voice. "She killed a *child*, yet there's still a bit of loyalty towards her. I must be rotten inside, just as bad as her."

"You've had the family thing hammered into you for years. It'll take a while to see things differently. Maybe even years. It takes a while to heal from that sort of shit."

"S'pose. I started seeing a therapist last week. I only did it because I wanted Hannah to go, too, so she could sort her head out. She never did like missing out on anything, so I thought she'd want to do it. It backfired, she said I was wasting my time. But I'm not. Janet, that's the therapist, I reckon she can fix me. I've got a way to go, I'm not all there up top, but at least I can admit that, unlike Hannah."

Two-Time picked his phone up and checked the local news site. He whispered close to her ear, "The fire's been reported." He showed her the screen.

An image of the burnt-out house sat beneath the headline: ARSON ON BRACKNELL. CHARRED BODY DISCOVERED. SQUATTER WAR?

Sienna relaxed a little. "At least that's us out of the picture for now."

"Our customers won't say anything, and besides, if they do, so what? We can deny we had anything to do with Hannah running the company. The police can't prove we worked for her. It's not like there's any paperwork, and we're paid in cash."

"There's the phones, though."

"Pay-as-you-go efforts. Our names aren't linked to them, and they're easily dumped."

"The Brothers are sorting it if we get grassed up. He's going to speak to his copper."

Sienna glanced at her phone. It had bleeped half an hour ago, and she hadn't dared check to see who it was. Didn't even want to. If George hadn't come up with the plan, she'd been willing to skip town for a bit and let them deal with Hannah on their own, but now, she'd made a promise to help them so they helped her in return.

She'd better see what her 'sister' wanted.

HANNAH: DON'T SPEAK TO ME LIKE THAT! HAVE YOU SORTED FINNEGAN YET?

SIENNA: SORRY, I WAS IN A GRUMP. I'M OKAY NOW. YEAH, ALL SORTED, BUT I THOUGHT IT WAS BEST TO GET RID OF ANY EVIDENCE THERE. I SET FIRE TO THE HOUSE.

HANNAH: WHAT? WHERE THE FUCK ARE WE MEANT TO WORK NOW?

SIENNA: IT'S FINE, I'VE FOUND SOMEWHERE.

HANNAH: I CAN'T BELIEVE YOU DID THAT. ARE YOU STUPID? WHAT IF CUSTOMERS COME FORWARD AND TELL THE POLICE WE'VE BEEN THERE?

SIENNA: THEY'RE TOO SCARED OF YOU TO DO THAT.

George had told her to big Hannah up, make her think she was the bee's knees. He'd said people with egos needed them fed regularly, and so long as Hannah thought she had the upper hand, everything would be all right.

HANNAH: TRUE, BUT THERE'S THE MATTER OF A DEAD BODY THAT'LL BE FOUND.

SIENNA: I'VE CHECKED. THE POLICE THINK HE WAS A SQUATTER. MAYBE THEY'LL PUT IT DOWN TO SOMEONE SETTING FIRE TO THE PLACE AFTER THEY'D KILLED HIM.

HANNAH: THEY'D BLOODY BETTER. I'M ON MY WAY HOME IN A TAXI. DONKEY FUCKED OFF. HE'S OUT OF THE TEAM NOW, I DON'T WANT HIM BACK, SO IF HE CONTACTS YOU, TELLS LIES ABOUT ME, IGNORE HIM.

Lies? She must mean the murder last night.

What had happened? Had Hannah and Donkey fallen out over it?

SIENNA: LIKE I'D BELIEVE ANYTHING BAD ABOUT YOU. HOW COME HE'S OFF THE TEAM?

HANNAH: IT DOESN'T MATTER. WHERE ARE YOU?

SIENNA: IN THE BELLS WITH TWO-TIME. I WOULD HAVE TOLD THE CUSTOMERS ABOUT THE NEW BASE BUT THOUGHT I'D BETTER LET YOU APPROVE IT FIRST.

HANNAH: GOOD. WE'LL GO LATER, WHEN IT'S DARK. ANYONE WHO NEEDS TO PAY UP BY TODAY CAN HAVE A REPRIEVE.

Surprised by Hannah's leniency, Sienna picked up the burner George had given her. Hannah coming home early might fuck everything up, so she'd better warn the twins.

SIENNA: SHE'S ON HER WAY HOME. WANTS TO SEE THE NEW LOCATION TONIGHT.

GG: FUCK'S SAKE. OKAY, I'LL LET YOU KNOW WHERE IT IS ONCE I'VE CLEARED IT OUT.

Sienna frowned. Decided she didn't want to know what he'd be clearing out and why. Maybe he had a house or flat somewhere and wanted his stuff gone before they played out the ruse.

SIENNA: SHE'S GOING TO WANT TO KNOW WHERE IT IS. WHAT DO I SAY?

GG: JUST TELL HER IT'S A LOCK-UP. TURN THE MESSAGE TONE AND VIBRATE OFF IN CASE SHE HEARS IT. DELETE THIS CONVERSATION. TALK LATER.

She did that and slid the burner in her pocket, her belly filled with butterflies. She'd told George about what Uncle Abel had said about them not being sisters, and they were going to look into it, see if there was any truth to the claim. What if it was true, though? What would she do then? Force Hannah to admit the truth?

"She's on her way home. Knows we're here." Sienna looked at Two-Time, seeing past the double scars, his scary façade. Why hadn't she seen the good in him before now? *Maybe because it was drilled into me to see the bad in everyone.* "She'll either tell me to go and meet her or she'll walk in here, so keep an eye out. We don't want her overhearing anything." She passed him her phone so he could read the message string.

"I bet Donkey was with her last night," he said.

"That's what I thought."

"Her whole world is tumbling down." He laughed. "About fucking time. Are you going to let people off, you know, wipe their debts when you take over?"

"No. I'm going to run the business my way, give them a longer time to pay. The twins are going to help me get the word out that they've got my back."

"Good. How are you going to handle her when she clocks your hair and whatnot?"

"Act like she's right, that I should go back to how I was before. Pacify her."

"It's not like you're going to have to do it for long, is it."

"No, because the grab will happen tonight now, I bet, not tomorrow."

They lapsed into silence for a while. Two-Time went to the bar and got another round in. Sienna pondered how her life would change, how, when she woke up in the morning, it would all be over. No more Hannah.

Two-Time came back and blew out a long breath. Was this getting to him?

"I wonder who my real mum and dad are," she said.

He sipped his pint. "Dunno. Would you want to meet them? What if they gave you up, you were adopted? They might not want to see you."

"I want to know who I *should* have been with, what my real family is like."

"*Shh*, she's just walked in."

Guilt heated Sienna's cheeks at the sight of Hannah coming towards them, her arm in a sling. Sienna hated these topsy-turvy emotions. Hated Hannah yet loved her. Wanted her dead yet didn't. Janet had better put her money where her mouth was and help Sienna get over this shit, because at the moment, she'd snapped right back into fear mode. How could just seeing someone who'd treated you badly do this? How could your resolve crumble just like that?

Conditioning, George had said.

Hannah plonked her arse on a short stool and raised her eyebrows at Two-Time. He got up, like he usually would, and went to buy her a drink. Seeing him obey without Hannah saying a word had Sienna so cross with herself. She could see it now, how the manipulation worked, how people like Hannah clicked their fingers and people jumped.

"How did the op go?" Sienna asked.

"They dug some flesh and bone out and used the flap of skin to cover it over. I was only out for an hour, so God knows what kind of hatchet job they did."

"Better than having to go to hospital, though."

"Yeah, but I'm three grand down. *That* pissed me off, so the woman who came round with Jackson's money can pay me back. It was her bloody fault I got shot in the first place."

Typical Hannah, not willing to admit she'd been the cause.

"How will you find her?" Sienna asked.

"Dunno, I'll think of something. Shame we don't have her address, else we could have got Two-Time to give her a visit." She leant forward. "I saw the news about the fire, on my phone. Read the article. You're right, they think two squatters had a barney. The neighbours said they'd seen two men coming and going. No mention of women. Still, don't get complacent. It was a stupid move on your part, and you need to be punished for it."

"Okay."

Hannah stared at her funny. "Okay?"

Sienna shrugged. "It's not like I can stop you cutting me, is it, and I fucked up, so I deserve what I get."

Hannah smiled. "Sounds like you've gone back to your normal self. Thank God for that. You've been doing my head in."

Two-Time came back and placed her vodka and tonic down. He sat, watching the pub, like she'd expect him to.

"So, what's this place you've got lined up?" Hannah gulped some of her drink.

"It's a lock-up. Like you said, we'll go tonight."

"Where is it?"

"I don't know. My contact hasn't said. Best not talk about it here, eh?"

"Why?"

"Because, like the house, it belongs to someone, it isn't used, and we don't want earwiggers listening in, do we? Half the scallies round here would go and claim it to store their hooky gear."

"Fair enough." Hannah sighed. "I'll drink this then go home for a kip. That bloody anaesthetic's wiped me out. I need a painkiller soon an' all. They charged me two hundred quid for those.

The prescription type. Fucking daylight robbery."

Sienna offered the required sympathetic noises, struggling with her see-saw feelings. She dragged up the image of a little girl being shot, and her empathy for Hannah dried up.

I have to remember she killed a kid. Treated me like shit.

It was the only way she'd get through this.

Chapter Thirteen

*V*alerie wasn't sure what to do. So much time had passed since Yvette had come to her with the news she was pregnant. The baby was three months old now. Little Sadie was cute and didn't look like her father, which was a bonus, and Yvette's life had been okay for the most part, although Valerie had slipped her a few quid here and there to help out, something she'd vowed not to do. When Bear had asked who'd got

Yvette pregnant, they'd blurted out a lie that she'd been raped, she didn't know who he was, he'd jumped her one night on her way back from the pub. Bear had swallowed it, had said it was too late to report it, and besides, they didn't need the police sniffing round the family, so the rape would be their secret.

The problem was, Yvette had been out on the piss last night, a friend of hers watching Sadie overnight, and Yvette had asked to meet up in the coffee shop this morning. She'd just told Valerie something that had turned her whole body cold, something Sadie's father had said to her in the pub.

"Word has it your sister and her fella are being naughty."

He walked off, leaving Yvette standing there, shitting herself.

She called out to him, "What? They're not doing anything!"

He turned and said, "Open your eyes, you dumb bitch."

"What the fuck do we do now? Jesus Christ," Valerie said, keeping her voice low. *"I* told *you something bad would happen because you'd been with*

him." She stared at Sadie in her pram. That kid was the biggest problem of all.

Yvette glanced around over both shoulders, then leant closer. "Look, 'being naughty' could mean anything. It doesn't necessarily point to anyone knowing about the loan shit."

"But if he knows, even if he has an inkling, he's going to bring trouble to my door, even if it's just to get back at you."

"For what? Being pregnant? As far as he's aware, I got rid of it. I'm no longer at the house, I live three fucking miles away from there, and I changed my job, so he can't even follow me anymore."

"He could have followed you last night. Did you walk or get a taxi?"

"Taxi, and I checked, no one was behind it."

"That's something, then. Listen, you're going to have to fix this, because if he turns up and it gets out you were seeing him, that he's Sadie's father, Bear's going to grill me about it, and I don't think I can lie to his face if he asks me outright."

"You're going to have to."

"No, you're going to stop it getting to that point. I'll watch Sadie tonight." Valerie bristled at that, seeing as a Saturday was her only night off, but what else could she do? "You're going back to that pub, and you're going to say it isn't me and Bear, that it's Tyke doing the lending, right?"

"Tyke?" Yvette laughed. "He wouldn't even lend his mum a fiver, let alone anyone else."

"That's not the point. We just need someone to blame it on."

"And you want me to go and say it. Great. That means seeing him again, and I don't want to. He scares me."

"He didn't scare you when you fucked him while you were unconscious, though, did he."

"That was below the belt. I had no control because I was unconscious."

"Sorry. You know, for saying that. I'm just frustrated. We've been at this for years, never had a whiff of trouble. All the customers are vetted, we're super bloody careful. And now look." Valerie paused as a thought came to mind. "I think he has been watching you. He's seen you come to ours, or worse, come to the office, and he's been clocking it all and decided he wants in on it. How else would he know?"

Yvette laughed wryly. "Do you think you're that scary, that your customers, if pushed, wouldn't admit what you're doing? You need to wake up, because if someone's got a knife to their throat, they're not going to let anyone slit it if they can help it. Someone's told him, and he's pissed off."

"Then do what I said and blame Tyke. We can't have him sniffing around, do you hear me?"

Dressed up for a night out, Sadie with Valerie, Yvette walked along Solomon Square and knocked on Twinkle's door. She'd trusted her friend with the identity of Sadie's father, if only so she had someone else to talk to about it. Valerie wasn't much cop in that regard, she wasn't interested in discussing it any more than she had to.

Twinkle was married to a man like Sadie's dad and Bear, domineering, always wanting it his way. While Twinkle and Yvette knew that kind of relationship wasn't right, neither of them had felt they could say no to their men. Valerie was just as bad by letting Bear boss her around, but she'd never admit it. Bear could be a right mean bastard when he had a mind, and Valerie, no matter what she said to the contrary, was wary of him. And Abel. She had to be, otherwise, why obey them all the time? Why let them walk all over her?

Maybe they weren't so different after all, Yvette and Valerie. The money, that must be why her sister hung around.

Twinkle opened the door and smiled, all tarted up for work. "Oh, hello, what are you doing here? I've got a customer due in half an hour."

Twinkle was a sex worker, and her husband, Chris, was her pimp. It was a weird setup, but it worked, as Twinkle liked what she did. That's what she said, but Chris being who he was, she likely didn't have a choice. They had kids together, too, and he always threatened to take them away from her if she stepped out of line.

"Is Chris home?" Yvette asked.

"No."

"Good. I just need…" Anxiety ramped up, and Yvette panicked. "Oh God, you've got to help me. Valerie's forcing me to do something, and I can't…I can't bloody do it."

Twinkle glanced up and down the street, looking for nosy neighbours. "Get in. I'll tell the punter he can't come until later."

Yvette rushed inside the clean and tidy house. It was silent, a cocoon. "Where are your boys?"

"Staying round Mum's. You know I don't entertain when they're here. What the fuck's wrong? You're in a right state."

174

They went into the kitchen, and Yvette sat at the table.

Instead of flicking the kettle on, Twinkle poured vodka and tonic, handing one to Yvette. "Looks like you need that. Get it down your neck and tell me what's going on. What's your sister forcing you to do? That fucking Valerie, she's so up her own arse. Thinks she's Queen Bee. All she does is lend money, for fuck's sake."

Yvette gulped the drink—she did need it—and launched into her tale. "So she said I need to go to the pub and blame Tyke. I mean, he's a little dick, but he doesn't deserve being framed, does he."

"No, he doesn't."

Yvette thought of her ex. "I don't want to see him *again."*

"I don't blame you, not after how he treated you, but... I have to say, you were a bit thick, going to the pub last night. Somewhere he drinks. Why not go to one round your area?"

"It was a pub crawl. My workmates, I was with them and didn't feel I could say no."

"Then you should have gone home. You've hidden from him all this time, he doesn't even know you had Sadie, and going there was inviting trouble."

"I know that now."

"In future, stay away. Shit, I need to ring my punter, I bloody forgot. Hang on." She went out into the hall to use the phone.

Twinkle's mum having her boys overnight had Yvette wishing her own mother was still alive. She'd have helped her out, encouraged her to move away from London, or even just to another leader's estate so there was no chance of bumping into that bastard. And what got Yvette the most was she was having to bail Valerie out of the shit. Why couldn't Bear go to the pub, saying he'd heard a rumour he was supposed to be running a loan shop and it wasn't him, he wanted to put the record straight?

Why does it have to be me?

Twinkle came back and leant on the worktop. "Listen, I don't think you should do what Valerie wants. This is her problem, not yours. She's only sending you because she thinks you have no choice. You've told her who Sadie's father is, so she's got you over a barrel now. She could go and tell him you didn't have an abortion, and she knows you won't want her to do that. I know she's your sister, but she's a scheming cow. The stories I've heard about her being nasty to people who don't pay up…"

"She doesn't do that, it's Abel."

"She's lying to you. Ask her about holding Molly Flint down for him while he cut her stomach."

The idea of that had Yvette wanting to throw up. "What?"

"Hmm, despite how tough she thinks they all are, how they're so scary no one would cross them, people are talking. That's how he's found out, because they've been going too far with the scare tactics. They should have just kept it to beating people up a bit, not this using knives shit."

"She wouldn't… She's not like that."

"There's a side to her you've got no clue about. She reminds me of how Myra Hindley was with that Brady fucker. She'll do whatever Bear says. You only see what you want to see, but I'm telling you… And no offence, although you're likely to take it, you're too naïve sometimes, come across as a bit thick up top."

"That's going a bit far."

"Sorry, but no one else is going to point it out to you, and I'm only doing it because I care. Fucking wake up, will you? Jesus, you got involved with a devious bastard, you had his kid against his wishes, and your sister is a cruel bitch who hurts people and enjoys it. Don't go to the pub."

"But…"

Twinkle hand-chopped the air to cut her off. "D'you know what I'd do in your shoes? Go and get Sadie, pack a suitcase, and piss off to a cheap hotel until you find somewhere else to live. Chris will collect the stuff from your flat. Start again elsewhere, because I promise you, your sister will get found out, so will Bear and Abel."

"I can't…"

"You can, you just don't want to. What's there to stick around for?"

"Valerie, and there's Hannah…"

"Excuses, that's all they are, and you've told me you think Hannah's a weird little cow, so she's no reason to stick around. If you loved Sadie, you'd get her the hell away from any fallout, because shit's going to go down, believe me."

"Not if Tyke gets the blame. Anyway, you can talk. Chris makes you have sex to earn money. Is that not devious, too?"

Twinkle sighed. "There's a difference. I agreed to it. I bloody like it, warped as that may be. Your fella, well, you didn't exactly like the drug night, did you?"

"Suppose not."

"You're going to do it your way no matter what I say, I'm wasting my sodding breath, but for the record, I think you're stupid getting involved in this. Your *part is over, you've been dumped and you're moving on. Your sister's shit is her issue. Now give me a hug and do what you've got to do, but don't come back to me expecting sympathy when it all goes tits up, because all you're going to get is 'I told you so.'"*

The pub was packed. He was nowhere to be seen, until he was, standing there staring at her, his face showing his displeasure. Someone was with him, a man. Her stomach rolled over, and she had the urge to run, to go and tell Valerie to sort her own mess out.

He came towards her, gripped her wrist, and propelled her to a corner.

"Stop coming in here," he said, close to her ear, his breath hot on the shell.

That used to turn her on, but now it revolted her. "I've…I've got to tell you something."

"There's nothing you could say that I'd want to hear. We're over, have been for ages. Jesus, I've fucked four women since you."

Was that supposed to hurt? It didn't. She was glad his attention had been elsewhere, but she felt sorry for those poor cows who'd been taken in by him. If she had the guts, she'd spread a rumour about what he'd done to her so women steered clear.

"It's about what you said to me last night."

His eyebrows shot up, and a crafty sneer transformed his face. "Oh, got some info for me, have you? I've been thinking about it a lot, and I wouldn't mind getting in on the action. Go out the back, into the yard. I'll meet you there in a few."

He let her go, and she walked off calmly, although she wanted to run. In the yard, she practised what she was going to say, repeating it over and over, making up a story she thought he'd believe. She couldn't have him questioning Tyke, it would become clear that he wasn't involved if that happened, but would her bullshit work? She had to try, Valerie was relying on her. Once this was done, she'd do what Twinkle had said. Get out of the East End. Go south, maybe, or north. West was too expensive for her, so that wasn't even on the table. Maybe Valerie and Bear would let her take out a loan so she could pay a bond and the first month's rent for a private place. Waiting to swap her council flat for another could take ages, and she just wanted a clean break.

The door opened, and she jumped, expecting to see just him, but he had a bloke with him. The door closed, and he backed her up against the wall.

"What's so important, then?" he asked.

His erection pressed into the top of her leg, and she forced back a gag.

"I asked my sister about the rumours."

"And?"

"It isn't them."

He belted out a nasty laugh. "Of course she'd say that."

"No, it's someone else. She went to him for a loan, and he said if she ever fucked him about over paying it back, he'd get word out that she was the one lending money. He said, 'I'll tell everyone, including Cardigan, it's you.'"

"And did she fuck him about?"

Yvette nodded. "She was a few hours late with the last payment. That was on Tuesday. He's done what he said, and now people think she's a bloody loan shark on Cardigan turf."

"Little bastard."

"And get this. He said if he was ever asked about it, he'd lie until he was blue in the face. Said something like: 'Cardigan will believe me. He wouldn't think someone like me would run a loan shop.'" She paused. "He's taking the piss, thinks he'll never get caught. If it was me, I'd just kill the fucker, wouldn't even question him."

She held her breath.

He stroked her face. "Did you get that abortion?"

The change of subject jolted her, and he'd said it in front of that bloke. Did he know about their relationship? Why was he even here? As a witness to what she'd said?

"Answer me," he ordered.

Shit. What should she do? "I...I couldn't bear to do it."

"Why did't you have one? I fucking told you it was the best way to go."

The fist to her stomach came as a massive shock. She doubled over, coughing, spluttering, and he dragged her away from the wall, letting her go. The momentum sent her to the ground, and he put the boot in, kicking everywhere, but the strike to the head hurt the most. It jarred her bones, clacked her teeth together, and she bit into her tongue. The taste of copper, the flood of warm, wet heat, then another two kicks to the head.

Everything went strange. She had her eyes open but couldn't see anything but blackness. She felt pain but it was dulled, as if her body had gone numb to protect her from the agony.

"Get rid of her," he said, delivering the last kick to her temple.

She hovered on the cusp of dropping into unconsciousness, desperate to stay alive for Sadie but wanting the comforting softness of oblivion at the same time. She could go to sleep for a bit, couldn't she? She'd wake up.

Wouldn't she?

Chapter Fourteen

George stood in the lock-up with Greg who cradled his jaw, complaining the painkillers were wearing off.

"Put a nappy on and shit in it while you're at it," George said.

"What?"

"You're acting like a baby."

"Bog off." Greg's speech was back to normal, thank God. "What are you going to do with him?" He pointed at Pete, still out of it from the sedative. "Take him to the warehouse and get rid of him? And what the fuck have you done to his *face*?"

George glanced at the skin ribbons hanging from the string. The fly still buzzed. "I was having a bit of fun."

"*Fun*? Sodding hell…"

George didn't fancy a lecture so aimed to steer Greg's thoughts elsewhere. "We'll take him to the warehouse now."

He got on with clearing out the lock-up, all the things he'd brought here: the chair, the upturned crate, the skin and string, the pegs. He dumped them in the back of the work van they'd opted to drive and went back to collect Pete, securing his wrists and ankles with cable ties, just in case. He lobbed him in the van, locked the doors, and whistled for Greg to get a move on.

Lock-up secure, George drove away. "Now that we've got Hannah to deal with, and the bloke she took with her to kill Libby, Pete's become a bit player, so I'll chop him up with the saw while he's asleep and dump him tonight when it's dark."

"Good, because keeping him as a plaything is a bit sick, even for you."

"I was going to enjoy myself with him for days, but oh well."

Greg gave him a sideways glance. "I worry about you."

"Don't bother. I'm never going to change."

The phone rang, and Greg put it on speaker. "Yep?"

"It's Mason."

"Right," George said, not surprised their PI had got back to them so quickly. "Any news?"

"You could say that. I've had a few people in the relevant places doing some digging, and from patching all the info together so far, Sienna definitely isn't Hannah's sister."

"Bugger. Go on."

"There's no mention of Hannah's mum, Valerie, having a second kid, although there *is* a birth certificate for a Sadie Weggley."

"Same surname as Hannah."

"Yes. The father has been left blank. The mother is listed as Yvette Weggley. Further poking around revealed she's Valerie's sister."

"Fuck me," George said. "So Valerie took on her niece, changed her name, and passed her off as her own?"

"Looks like it."

"That's not unheard of. People used to do that shit all the time. The amount of mums who are really nans…"

"Yeah, but why would she take the kid on?" Mason asked. "There's no death certificate for Yvette, and her last visit to the doctor was to get antibiotics for an ear infection after Sadie was born. Since then, nothing."

"Maybe she couldn't handle parenthood and Valerie agreed to bring the kid up."

"That's plausible, but there's no financial footprint after June fifth when Sadie was three months old. Her bank account's still got fifty-five quid in it."

"So you're suggesting she went missing."

"Yeah," Mason said, "but what if it wasn't legitimate?"

George had to admit, it did sound iffy. "I'll ask our copper. I wonder if they got a fake birth certificate with Valerie's and her fella's names on it. I mean, it'd be a big question to answer when

Sienna was old enough to get a copy of one if they refused to give her the original."

"I could poke about and see if any forgers from back then are still around, but I might need a few days for that."

"Don't bother, it's easily discovered by Sienna telling us what her certificate says, if she even has one. What I'm interested in is, if Yvette *is* missing, let's say dead, why was she killed?"

"I've still got info to come in, so I'll keep you posted."

"Cheers."

Greg swiped the screen. "From what Sienna told us, her supposed parents weren't married, so that explains why Hannah's called Weggley. Yvette clearly wasn't married either. What could have happened for the sisters to fall out enough that Yvette was killed?"

George chuckled. "So you're going down the sinister route like Mason?"

"Best to do that and work our way backwards."

"You're thinking Valerie did it?"

"Maybe."

"She might not have. What if Valerie's bloke did it? Or Yvette's, if she had one? Sienna's father? Or it could have been someone else entirely and they found out and took the baby on, like most people would do."

"Where's the body, though? Why would you hide a murder if you weren't involved? And no financials, it's bothering me."

"Yvette might not even have copped it. She could have changed her name, started again elsewhere. Message Janine, see if she can look into it for us. Even knowing whether there was a missing person report will help. Saying that, we could ask Hannah later. She might sing if we apply enough pressure." George parked in front of the warehouse, got out, locked the gate, and headed to the door.

Greg came up behind him, the phone ringing. "It's Janine. She's obviously okay to talk."

"Wait until we're inside before you answer that." George prodded the keypad, and the door swung inwards.

Inside, they sat on the sofa.

"All right?" Greg said upon answering, putting it on speaker.

"Bloody hell, I was just about to hang up," Janine griped. "Took you long enough."

Greg pulled a face. "Keep your hair on."

"I'm trying to fudge this investigation for you, in case you'd forgotten, so I'm a bit stressed. What do you want?"

George took over. "We need to know if there's a missing person file for a woman called Yvette Weggley, in the nineties. I haven't got a specific date as I don't know how old a certain person is to work it out."

"I'm not at the station, so you'll have to wait. What do you need to know for?"

"Nothing you need to concern yourself with. How's it going?"

"Not good. Well, good for you because there's nothing but dead ends, but not good for me because if I don't get the dad to admit something dodgy has been going on, my boss will be on my back. Is there anything you can tell me about why the killer went to the Nivens' place? I've got the father, Dillon, telling me he doesn't know why someone would have asked for him, not someone with a gun anyway, and I don't believe him. His kid's dead, yet he's covering up for someone."

"He owed money."

"How much?"

"No idea, but I can find out."

"Ask what it was for. That might shed some light on why he's being cagey."

"The person he borrowed it from must have decided she didn't want to wait for him to pay up."

"So, a loan shark? It's a woman, so it doesn't take a rocket scientist. It's one of the Weggleys, I bet. We've long suspected they're up to something."

George sighed. "And you didn't think to inform us? Cheers for that." He let the sarcasm hang in the air for a second. "It's Hannah, but for God's sake, keep that quiet. Sienna came to us for help."

"So she wasn't there?"

"No. I recruited one of their henchmen earlier, goes by the name of Two-Time."

"Him with the scarred face?"

"That's the one. I wanted him to spy on them, but the shit hit the fan. He said he didn't go with Hannah last night so it must have been a bloke called Donkey."

"Oh, that prat." Janine scoffed. "He's got a few priors for violence. I remember him being brought in about three years ago, kicking up a fuss when he was booked in. Clocked the desk sergeant on the chin."

"There's something else you should know. That house fire today…"

"Oh God, was that you?"

"No. The body belongs to some prat called Finnegan. Once he's put on the slab, the pathologist will see he's been shot."

"*That* was you, wasn't it."

"It was."

"*Christ*, George! What the *hell* are you involved in?"

"Like I said, we're helping Sienna. It started off as helping Genevieve, one of Debbie's girls, but it's all gone a bit tits up. One thing led to another, and here we are."

"What about the bullet?"

"I used a new gun. Well, it's been used abroad, if you catch my drift, and it was one of a few we bought recently."

"That could come in handy if the ballistics come up for another murder. You're a jammy bastard."

"Not really. Someone's picked the casings and bullets up. Anyway, when you get a minute, have a look into Yvette Weggley for us."

"Right. Now I've got to work out whether to let Nivens know I'm aware of what's been going on or keep it quiet. Get *him* to keep quiet."

"Our date with Hannah is going to be sooner than we thought, if that helps your decision. She's left the clinic, and we'll be picking her up later."

"Okay. I've got to go."

Greg put the phone in his pocket. "We'd better get that prick out of the van."

George nodded. "No rest for the wicked. I'll get him. You message Two-Time. Ask him why Nivens borrowed that money. We might be going down the rabbit hole with it, but I'm interested to know if there's something buried in a warren underground."

"Metaphor monster."

"Dick."

Hannah had left the Bells. Two-Time and Sienna had immediately switched their burner phones on in case the twins had sent any messages.

GG: WHY DID NIVENS BORROW MONEY, AND HOW MUCH?

Two-Time showed her the screen.

"Um, he's been using expensive escorts," she said. "Borrowed ten grand but had almost paid it off."

"Fucking hell. Can you imagine him having to tell his wife their kid got offed because of him seeing sex workers?"

TWO-TIME: PROSTITUTES. HIGH-END. TEN K.

GG: CHEERS.

Two-Time frowned. "Wonder why they wanted to know that?"

"Maybe it's for their copper."

Two-Time shrugged. "Probably."

Janine whistled at the words on her screen. No wonder Nivens had wanted to keep that snippet to himself. For him to have borrowed that much, he was going for the type of woman who charged a fortune by the hour.

Once Hannah's body and gun were in the mix, she'd have to go round there and query why a loan shark had been at their door. The reason for borrowing the money didn't matter, the fact he'd kept information from them did, and that was something he could be rapped on the knuckles for.

What he'd done didn't affect the twins, or her, so she wouldn't bother giving him a heads-up. Maybe, when it came out that the killer was a loan shark, Nivens would have the sense to say it was a case of mistaken identity, Hannah had gone to the wrong house.

Then again, Nivens' financial records would be gone through, and any anomalies flagged, like why he'd perhaps drawn chunks of money out to pay Hannah back.

Either way, he was in the shit with his wife.

Not my circus.

Chapter Fifteen

*V*alerie hadn't expected to see a man on the doorstep, holding Yvette in his arms and looking grim.

"I don't know what the fuck is going on," he said, "and I don't want to, but she's just had a serious kicking, and I've been told to get rid of her. You deal with her."

Valerie thought about Bear, the fallout, the risk to their business, how this simple mission had gone so bloody wrong. And the state of Yvette…fucking hell, her face was a mess of blood and bruises. "I can't take her to a hospital, there'll be too many questions."

"Say she managed to get here and must have been beaten up."

Valerie's ears buzzed with panic. "But what if she says otherwise when she wakes up?"

"Jesus. Right, let me think… Okay, there's this place, on Moon's estate." He told her the address. "Go there. They won't turn you away so long as you've got the money to pay for her to get patched up."

Bear came up behind Valerie and stared over her shoulder. "What the bloody hell?"

"Take her," the man said. "I don't reckon she's got long, she got kicked in the head one too many times, so if you don't hurry up…"

Bear nudged Valerie out of the way and took Yvette. "Who did this to her?"

The visitor grimaced. Shrugged. He walked down the path, got in his car, and drove off.

Bear turned to Valerie. "She's half fucking dead! Did her rapist do this? Has he been watching her all this time, waiting, and then beat the shit out of her?"

Valerie swallowed, fear gripping her tummy—and her tongue, it seemed. She didn't know what to bloody say, until, "Christ. Oh God. Oh fuck. Um…um, she needs to go to this clinic he said about. Err, there's Hannah and Sadie…we can't just leave them. Abel's not here to babysit."

Bear shook his head. "Then I suppose I'll have to fucking deal with her, won't I. This is meant to be our night off, the only one we get a week, yet here I am, sorting out your sister's mess."

"You'll need money. He said…he said you'll need money."

Valerie rushed into the living room, ignoring Hannah who watched the telly. Sadie slept soundly on the sofa, swaddled in a blanket. Valerie dived for the money holdall and took a couple of bundles out. Would two grand be enough? It sounded like the clinic was private, so would they want more?

She ran outside to where Bear loaded Yvette into the back of the car.

He closed the door and snatched the cash off her. "What's she been doing, other than getting herself raped, to have been beaten up?"

"I don't know! Maybe she got caught up in something at the pub and there was a fight." She glanced into the car but couldn't see Yvette in the

199

darkness. "Fuck arguing about it, just get her to that clinic."

"Where is it?"

She rattled off the location, and he stomped to the driver's seat and got inside, the window rolling down.

"Get Abel round here," Bear snapped. "I've decided I'm not dealing with this bullshit by myself, so use his car and meet me there. She's your *sister, not mine."*

He sped off, and she ran indoors to use the phone, shaking all the way to her toes, because if she hadn't sent Yvette to that pub, none of this would be happening.

"Do you like the baby?" Uncle Abel asked Hannah from his perch on the armchair by the window.

He peered out every so often, probably waiting for Mum and Dad to come back. He drank lager from a tall can, letting out little burps. He wasn't her real uncle, just Dad's best mate, but it didn't matter. Hannah liked him, but he was a bit weird sometimes. He looked at her funny on occasion, as if she were a puzzle, someone he had to work out. She reckoned she was. A puzzle. She even confused herself every now and then. She was a girl, and as such, she was supposed to play with dolls, to like the colour pink, to want to have her hair all pretty, but she didn't.

Inside, she was angry, nearly all the time. She had to pretend to be like everyone else, and it was hard work. Something wasn't right, but she didn't know what. Her brain, there was a problem with it. She couldn't tell Dad, else he'd say she had to buck up and stop being a prat, and Mum would say she loved Hannah just as she was, so there was nothing to worry about.

Except there was. Hannah had horrible thoughts. They were the sort that belonged in nightmares, where monsters, hidden inside human bodies, ran round hurting people, using machetes to chop their feet off so they couldn't escape. Blood, everything was the colour of blood, her visions viewed through a crimson lens. They appeared in her mind if someone annoyed her, or if she got in trouble at school. The only way she could get back at people was to imagine killing them, then she felt better.

That wasn't normal, was it?

"Did you hear me?" Abel said.

"Uh?" Hannah blinked. Recalled the question he'd asked. "She's all right."

A lie.

She stared at Sadie, the yellow waffle blanket wrapped tightly around the little body. Mum said babies slept better that way. Swaddling, she'd called it. Auntie Yvette didn't do that, then complained Sadie hardly slept. Auntie was always ignoring good advice, so Mum said.

"All right?" Abel chuckled. "She's going to be trouble. For all of us."

A worm wriggled in Hannah's belly, and her lens grew red around the edges. Oh God, she was going to have one of those horrible episodes. "How come?"

Abel gave her a mysterious glance then nosed back out of the window. "Let's just say we might be seeing more of her than we'd like."

In a vision, she saw herself sitting on Sadie's face until she stopped breathing. "Has Mum said she'll look after her when Auntie Yvette's at work or something?"

There had been a discussion about that, Dad saying he needed Mum with him at their job, so she couldn't watch the baby, Mum agreeing; she didn't want the responsibility, and Yvette had made her own bed and had to lie in it, whatever that meant.

Abel rubbed his cheek. "No, she hasn't, but things might change, considering what's happened tonight."

More crimson, Sadie's lips turning blue.

Hannah sort of had an idea what Abel meant. A man had brought Auntie Yvette here, and Dad had taken her to a clinic, then Abel had come, and Mum had dashed off, too, saying she'd be back as soon as she could and sorry for the trouble.

"The clinic will fix her," Hannah said, and the lens cleared a bit. She sighed with relief.

"By the sound of it, it might be too late."

Unease crept inside her. "What do you mean?"

"Yvette might die, then Sadie will need someone to look after her."

Hannah folded her arms and glared at the baby. She didn't want her living with them, she cried when she was hungry, and her nappies smelled really bad. Mum gave her loads of attention, and it meant Hannah felt left out.

"So," Abel said. "Do you like the baby?"

Hannah's face flamed, as did her vision. "No."

He smiled. "Neither do I, kid."

The rage built, and she struggled to keep her emotions in check. "I wish she was dead. I wish she'd never been born." It was the first time she'd admitted that to anyone, and far from being ashamed, she was relieved at getting it out of her head.

"If the worst comes to the worst and she has to live with you, there are ways to make her behave. I used to do it to my wife when she was alive."

Hannah tensed. "Are you talking about hurting Sadie's belly?" She had overheard a chat about that, and she'd gone to bed thinking about doing it to the mean girls at school.

"How do you know about that?" Abel frowned.

"You lot don't talk quietly."

He laughed, the sound low. "Suppose not. But yeah, we could hurt her belly. Not until she's older, though."

Hannah knew she shouldn't want to, that it was wrong, but like she'd thought earlier, something wasn't right with her brain, and she visualised cutting Sadie's stomach, her podgy baby stomach that Auntie Yvette blew raspberries on.

"We can't tell anyone, though," Abel said.

"But Sadie might. When she's older, she'll be able to talk."

Abel smiled, showing his large front teeth. "Ah, but by then, she'll be able to understand that she mustn't breathe a word about it."

"How do you know I won't?"

"Because if you do, I'll tell people it was you, I had nothing to do with it, then you'll go into a care home."

Bubbles of fear popped in her gut, and her whole view turned red. If she wasn't careful, if she didn't control it, she'd roll over onto the baby right now and suffocate her. It wasn't like she could go outside and kick a cat to calm her down, was it. "That's not nice."

"No, it isn't." He grinned wider. "And neither am I. Now then, it's time for bed. Go and get your pyjamas on and brush your teeth." He reached for the remote and switched the telly over.

Hannah looked at the baby. "I don't want to miss it, so you won't cut her belly while I'm gone, will you?"

"Nah. Like I said, she needs to be older for that."

She left the room, confused by the excitement fizzling inside her.

No, she most definitely wasn't normal.

The scent of antiseptic would always remind Valerie of this night. Of death. Of fear. Of guilt. Yvette had died just before Valerie had arrived, and she currently lay in a private room. She looked as if she just slept, and if it wasn't for the awful, awful bruises and other injuries, no one would know she'd had the kicking of her life.

Her nose was broken. Her eyelashes had turned inwards, hidden by what the doctor had called oedema. Yvette had a swelling to her brain, and the kicks to her head had been too much for her to pull through. Her whole face was like a football, a big, swollen mess, the skin so tight it seemed it might split. Her lips had puffed up, one with a nasty gash, and her jaw appeared to be unhinged, the bottom veering off to the left.

I've done this. I sent her to that pub. To save myself and Bear. To hide what we've been doing.

In this stark reality, it didn't seem important anymore, the money lending, the secrets. Yvette had died for something Valerie had willingly walked into, she'd paid the price Valerie should have, and nothing would make it right.

Until Yvette had met that bastard, she'd never understood Valerie's obsession with Bear, how she'd blindly done whatever he wanted. But she'd certainly known by the time that man had finished with her — how could she not if she'd allowed him to pay her like a slapper and give her drugs, doing whatever he wanted to her?

Sadie. What the fuck were they going to do about her? Valerie didn't want her, much as she thought the baby was a little darling. If she'd wanted another kid she'd have had one. Hannah was enough, thank you, but on the other hand, how could she take Sadie on? How would she explain where Yvette was?

And the body, this shell that remained of her sister. What was going to happen about that? They'd come to the clinic because the man had said so. In the face of Yvette being dead, it seemed such a simple thing now, getting out of the shit. They could have taken her to an NHS hospital after all, said she'd been beaten up and had managed to get to Valerie's, which had been discussed on the doorstep, but at the time it had seemed the wrong path to take.

The doctor here had asked what they wanted to do. Alert the authorities about the death or…oh God…the body could be destroyed without anyone knowing about it.

For a price.

"What should we do?" she asked Bear who sat in the comfy chair beside the bed.

"We don't need any questions, do we," he said. "We protect the business at all costs."

"The business is why this happened," she ground out.

"What?"

She'd have to come clean. "She was doing me a favour. Last night, she heard that people have been talking about us, whispering shit they shouldn't be whispering. I sent her back there tonight to say Tyke's been lending money, not us. If I hadn't done that, she'd still be alive."

"But we might not be. If Cardigan finds out what we've been up to..."

She should have known he'd be blunt about it. He'd never liked Yvette, so what did he care whether she'd snuffed it. So long as he was safe, his precious business, that was all that mattered to him. She should have left him long ago, as soon as he'd started being nasty to Hannah, treating her poorly. Now, their child was a mirror image of him, a spiteful girl who was only out for herself. He'd moulded her, and Valerie dreaded to think what Hannah would be like as an adult.

"Like I just said, what do we do?" She bit her lip, already knowing the answer.

"We let the clinic deal with the body. Pay them whatever it takes."

"What about Sadie?" She prayed he'd say they'd give her up to social services.

"Don't you want her?"

She wasn't even ashamed to admit it. "No."

"That's just tough."

Her stomach flipped. "What are you saying, that we have to take her on?"

"Yep."

"Why?" she whined and sounded like Hannah, a brat who wanted her own way.

"Think about it. If we rock up to social services, saying her mother upped and left, they're going to tell the police, who'll look into it, try to find her, ask questions. People are going to say she was in the pub. Some might even grass on the fella who kicked her about. Then what? No, we can't risk plod coming to us. We'll keep Sadie and pretend she's ours."

"It's not going to work."

"Why not?"

"Because people know she isn't ours."

Bear shrugged. "Then we'll move house. I don't fucking know."

"But her birth certificate—"

"We'll get a new one off Dodge."

She thought of the forger. "Will he keep quiet, though, for something as big as this?"

"If we pay him double." Bear rubbed his forehead. "Tonight's turned out to be well expensive."

"I can't believe you just said that when my sister's right there, dead."

"Listen to me, you. Emotions can't come into it. You've got to forget she's carked it and face facts. I don't want the bobbies sniffing around, and I certainly don't want to give the business up, which we'd have to

209

if Tyke doesn't get the blame and people are still spouting that it's us. Cardigan will be after our arses. How do we even know Yvette managed to plant that seed about Tyke? We don't. Maybe this was for the best. It's forcing us to be more careful. We'll change offices an' all. Arrange meetings with new borrowers in cafés and shit so there's no specific location for them to tell anyone about. We'll use mobile phones different to our usual ones. It just needs a bit of thinking put into it, and we'll be golden."

Golden. It was all black as far as Valerie was concerned. Yvette was dead. There was a baby in the family Valerie didn't want to raise. Then there was a house move on the cards.

She stared at Yvette and cursed her to Hell and back.

Why did she have to go and fucking die?

He stood outside the ex-servicemen's club on Daltrey Road with his mate. He kept his dalliances with females to himself, there was an agreement between him and the women every time. He didn't want people knowing he played around. Tyke needed sorting, and he didn't want to get his hands dirty,

hence his mate being here. He could force Tyke to let him in on the business, but no, he couldn't be bothered.

He believed Yvette's explanation, even though she'd lied to him about the abortion. Giving her a kicking had calmed him down. Now, he saw things in a different light. She could have the kid for all he cared, she just needed to keep his name out of it and not expect him to dip into his pocket for a bastard he hadn't wanted. The earlier beating should be a good enough warning.

Now the anger had cleared with the rumour being false, he didn't really think Valerie and Bear had the balls to run a loan operation. They were a pair of bumbling idiots, and it was just Tyke's style to tell them he'd blame it on them. Prick.

"Go and get him," he said. "I'll wait round the back."

"Right."

His friend lumbered inside.

I really don't need this shit, but it'll be all over after tonight.

He walked down the side of the club and waited by the rear yard gates. Opposite, tatty scrubland, and beyond, the edge of a housing estate. The homes stood in darkness bar the fuzzy dots of streetlamps and the glows in windows.

"What the fuck are you doing? Get your hands off me!" Tyke's voice, faint, from the front of the club.

Footsteps. The sounds of a scuffle.

"Look, I can walk by myself. You don't need to hold my arm, all right? Fucking hell. And it would be nice to know what this is about."

They rounded the corner, and he watched their approach. His mate stopped and pushed Tyke against the tall gates, his hand at his throat.

"Oi, there's no need for this. What the fuck have I done?" Tyke wheezed.

He stepped forward. Nodded to his mate and walked away. Waited on the corner with his back to the scene.

The thud of punches. The scrape of feet on the path. The 'oof' of Tyke's breath being punched out of him.

He looked forward to getting alcohol down his neck once they'd dumped the body. He glanced over his shoulder. Tyke on the ground, strangulation in progress.

Wanker.

Bear had returned home to collect more money, then had gone back to the clinic to hand it over. The doctor had spoken to Moon who'd agreed Yvette could be

transported that night to an undertaker who, for a grand, would put her inside someone else's coffin that was bound for the crematorium in the morning.

Bear had dropped Valerie home, telling her to contact Dodge and get the ball rolling on a birth certificate. Tomorrow, they'd look for somewhere else to live, clear out Yvette's flat, and send a letter on her behalf to the council saying she was giving up her tenancy.

He jogged to the pub and got pissed up over the next two hours, drowning his sorrows, his life ripped out at the roots, those roots to be replanted fuck knew where.

"If only she'd stayed in that coma, got better," he mumbled. "But no, she didn't come out of it, she died, for fuck's sake. Things have got to change. We need to be more careful."

"What was that?" an old man beside him asked.

"Nothing." Bear downed another drink. "Nothing."

Chapter Sixteen

Night-time had rolled around too quickly for Sienna's liking. She'd suggested they wait until around eleven, so it got proper dark. George had given her the location of the lock-up, and they were on the way there, Hannah in the passenger seat, Two-Time in the back. Nerves frazzled, Sienna tried to calm herself down. She didn't need Hannah picking up on her anxiety.

"So we've got six months at the new place before it all gets demolished," Hannah checked.

"That's what my contact told me." Sienna prayed Hannah wouldn't ask who that was.

"And their name is…?"

Shit. "John someone or other. I heard him talking about the demolition in the pub. He's in charge of cleaning the lock-ups out, making sure no squatters get in, which is why he was able to give us the keys."

"When did you get them off him?"

"I didn't, they're under a rock outside our unit. I gave him a grand for helping us out. I assumed that would be okay with you."

"From the stash at the loan house?"

"Yeah."

"And where is that money now?"

"In my flat." *And I'm going to keep the fucking lot.*

Hannah took a deep breath. "I don't like not being in the know from the off. It makes me uneasy. Dad taught me to be on the ball at all times."

"It's only this once I'll have taken charge. You *were* having an operation. You can't be expected to be in two places at once." God, Sienna hated pandering to Hannah, but it wouldn't be long now, and she'd never have to do it again.

"I suppose." Hannah stared out of the window.

Sienna drove past a row of garages, then down a track between them, coming out to where the lock-ups were. George had said the one they wanted was the only one without a padlock, and of course, there was the rock, which turned out to be a lump of concrete.

She parked, the headlamps lighting up the blue door. "It's that one."

"Two-Time, get out and check everything's all right," Hannah ordered. "Go inside. Walk round the back first. I'm not getting out until I know it's safe."

He left the car, no sign he was pissed off with her demand. He was playing his part well, and Sienna could only assume she was doing the same. Hannah hadn't looked at her funny or anything.

Sienna breathed out slowly, not wanting her relief to show. She'd been dreading this bit. George had said it would be easier if he hid behind the lock-ups until everyone else was inside. If Hannah had gone to do the checking, she'd have spotted him waiting in the darkness out of sight, then she'd have run, George chasing after her. 'Hassle', he'd called it, and he didn't want any of that.

"It's nice and abandoned," Hannah said. "No chance of people coming here off the cuff."

"Yep, it's a great location. We'll have Two-Time to deal with anyone who thinks it's a good idea to nick the money. Anyway, only the customers will know there's cash here, and they won't say anything. It'll be the same as at the house, just out of the way a bit."

"Hmm."

"And desperate people won't mind coming out here to collect their money." *Should I shut up? Am I babbling?*

"That's why the business does so well. People will go the distance for a bit of cash to get them out of the shit."

Sienna recalled Dad saying that. Hannah was him all over, had taken on his mantle. She was just as spiteful, too. Sienna hoped the twins found out who she really belonged to. If they came back and reported that she really was Valerie's and Bear's, she didn't know how she'd take it.

But why would Abel say we're not sisters if it isn't true?

"What are you thinking about?" Hannah asked. "You've gone too quiet for my liking."

"Nothing much."

Two-Time returned from his jaunt round the back, a thumb up to give the all-clear on that front. He bent to collect the key and stuck it in the padlock, pushing the door wide so Hannah could see inside. He flicked the light on and glanced at her.

She nodded. "That'll do. Plenty big enough."

She got out, and Sienna cut the engine. Hannah entered the lock-up, Two-Time going to stand in the middle. Sienna joined them, pocketing the car keys, nervous about the next step. About Hannah realising this had been a trap and Sienna had betrayed her.

Two-Time shut the door.

"Seeing as we've lost the table and chairs," Hannah said, "because *someone* set the house on fire, we're going to need a new set. We'll get one from that charity place in the morning."

Sienna ignored the jibe. It wouldn't be long, and she wouldn't have to hear them anymore. "Can we get a peephole this time?"

"Two-Time can just drill a hole. Then again, it's not going to do any good at night, is it? There's no streetlamps like at the house, so we won't see who's here anyway."

"Do you want me to take over Finnegan's role?" Two-Time asked. "Stay here with you two?"

Hannah pinched her chin. "Yeah, until we recruit someone else—I've only got you now to beat people up, seeing as Donkey's fucked off. And I want you to find that Scottish bastard and his sister. She owes me money for my op, and he owes me for the finger, *and* the money he took with him from Jackson. I reckon you could take him." She smiled at Two-Time. "You're both about the same size."

Was that the scrape of a foot outside?

"Well," Sienna said loudly, we'll be up and running again tomorrow, so if the Scot thought he could bring us down, he was wrong."

"I wonder where Jackson went," Two-Time said.

"I don't care about him." Hannah scratched her cheek. She pointed to the sling. "If he hadn't sent *her* round, this wouldn't have happened and Finnegan wouldn't be dead."

The door flew open, and, as planned, Two-Time took his gun out. Hannah backed against the side wall, Sienna doing the same but going opposite. Ginger George strode in, gun aimed at Hannah.

"Oh, for fuck's *sake*!" she shouted. "Will you just *fuck off*?"

"Afraid not," he said, Scottish accent thick.

Hannah skipped her attention to Two-Time. "Shoot the bastard, then!"

George pulled the trigger, the bullet entering Hannah's shin. She screamed, went down like a sack of shit, blood colouring her blue jeans. She slapped her free hand on the hole, then patted and checked her calf in a panic.

"Oh God, the bullet's stuck in my leg. Shit. Fuck."

"Shut up moaning," George said. For show, he swung the gun towards Two-Time. "Put your weapon down."

"Don't you dare," Hannah panted out. "Jesus Christ, my *leg*!"

"By all means," George said, "listen to her if you don't mind being dead, because I *will* shoot you like I shot that other drip...in the head."

"All right, all right." Two-Time lowered his gun to the floor.

"What are you *doing*?" Hannah barked. "Don't listen to him, listen to *me*."

Two-Time shook his head. "If I don't do what he wants, he'll shoot all of us. Let's see what he's after, negotiate. There's no need for more blood."

"Good man." George smiled. "Kick your gun over here."

It skittered across the floor.

George bent to pick it up. "Now then, we're going for a little drive." He dug in his pocket and threw cable ties on the floor. "You." He pointed to Sienna. "Cuff his hands behind his back."

"You're going to fucking pay for this," Hannah said. "I swear to God…"

"Shut *up*, woman." George jerked one of the guns at Sienna, the other trained on Two-Time. "Do it!"

Sienna, amazed everything was going to plan, snatched the ties up and did as he'd asked.

"Now cuff her." George cocked his head towards Hannah.

"Don't listen to him," Hannah said. "It's me you take orders from, no one else."

Sienna made a show of shaking. "He's got two guns. I have to do it. If we just...if we do as he says, everything will be okay." She looked at George. "What do you even want? Why are you here? Did you follow us?"

"Of course I fucking followed you. I've been tailing you all day. And I want money, everything you've got."

"No way." Hannah shook her head. "You're not robbing me. *Nobody* robs me."

"I think you'll find I am." George tightened his finger on the trigger. "You're minus a finger, you've got a bullet in your leg. Do you want another one somewhere else?"

"You bastard."

"That's the nicest thing anyone's ever called me."

Sienna went over and had to force Hannah to roll onto her side so she could cuff her. She crouched and did the cable tie up tight. "I'm sorry. I'm so sorry..."

She was and she wasn't. She was sorry it had come to this, that their lives had sent them in this direction, to this point, but it had to stop, the cutting, the manipulation, Hannah doing whatever she wanted because she had an inflated sense of entitlement.

"Wrestle him for a gun," Hannah whispered.

"What?" *She's prepared for me to get killed?* "He'll shoot me before I even get close."

"If you two think you can hatch some plan," George said, "don't bother." He whistled through his teeth.

Sienna stood. What was going on? George hadn't mentioned this bit.

Another man appeared, a ginger wig and beard on, gun in hand. He was identical to George. Sienna let out a nervous giggle.

"What the fuck?" Hannah stared between the two men. "Who the hell are *you*?"

Greg marched over, gripped Hannah's upper arm, and dragged her out as if she weighed nothing. Hannah screeched all the way, from anger and pain, her voice fading the farther Greg took her.

"Noisy cow." George tucked the guns away. He took a cable tie from his pocket. "Sorry, love, but needs must for appearance's sake until it's time for the big reveal."

Sienna turned so he could bind her wrists behind her. "Someone will come and get my car, won't they?"

"Yep, my man, Dwayne, is round the back. He'll drop it off at your flat. Since she's out of the way and can't see you, I won't put the blindfolds on until we're at the van. No sense in you tripping over, is there."

"You didn't mention blindfolds—or Greg coming," Sienna said.

"Look, I don't really know you from Adam. I can't trust you with the next location until I'm sure you won't go off and tell someone. It's where we do a lot of our nasty business. We've had it for years, and no one's ever blabbed where it is so far, and I'd like to keep it that way."

"Okay, okay…" Sienna said, the situation catching up with her. They were actually doing this, getting rid of Hannah, and she wasn't sure if she was elated or scared of what was to come.

George's question in the parlour came back to her: *Are you killing her or am I?*

She'd answered, "I am."

Now, she wasn't sure she had the bottle. Would he mind if she backed out?

"Come on," he said.

Sienna stared at the blood on the floor. There would be more of that in her future, going by what George had said. Could her stomach handle it?

She killed a kid, she killed a kid…

It would have to.

The place was massive. George had taken Sienna's blindfold off, and, sitting on a fold-out chair, she gazed around to acclimatise. Ahead, the back of a sofa, a big flatscreen in front of it. To her left, a door she assumed they'd come through. The right, a weird rack on the wall, manacles, spikes. A quick glance over her shoulder revealed a long table with tools on top, and two doors.

On wooden chair, Hannah sat closest to the rack, blindfolded, a rag in her mouth, roped around her middle like Sienna and Two-Time. George had taken her sling off, and her bandaged hand hung steady. To Sienna's other side, also blindfolded, Two-Time clenched his teeth. For a moment, she doubted George. What if he'd tricked them and they were all going to be slaughtered? Was Two-Time thinking the same thing? Could they believe that when the twins gave their word, they'd stick to it?

George and Greg had removed their beards and wigs, George in a forensic suit and gloves, the hood down, his hands covered with blue gloves, Greg in a grey suit and red tie. It was obvious who they were, and Hannah would be under no illusion when her blindfold came off.

George pulled Two-Time's down past his chin and held both thumbs up, then raised a finger to his lips. *Shh.* He moved along to Hannah and yanked the material away from her eyes, bending to stare into them.

"All right, sunshine?"

She blinked, momentarily stumped as to why someone else was here, panic and shock blasting her features, then she screeched behind the rag, rearing her head back to get away from his face. It was the first time Sienna had seen her ruffled. Scared. Then she seemed to get a hold of herself and sneered.

"Welcome to the warehouse. I'm George, and this is Greg, also known as the ginger cunts. You want to kill us, don't you. I can see it in your eyes. The thing is, you can't, not roped to that chair, and your sidekicks are in a similar situation.

There's no escaping." He pulled the rag out, dropped it on the floor, and stepped back, fingers linked, twirling his thumbs over and over each other.

"What the fuck?" Hannah breathed heavily, her shoulders going up and down. "Where's that Scottish bloke gone? What is he, your heavy?"

"That was me," he said, changing his accent to Scottish. Then back to London with, "I've been watching you for a while. Pete Jackson pissed me off, so I followed him around from time to time. I won't bother going into it, there's no need. I've got what I want—you, with nowhere to run. I was naffed off about you running your business without permission, you know that because you had a warning. You ignored it, and that was enough for me to bring you in, but you've been up to much worse, haven't you, and that trumps a bit of money lending."

Hannah's eyebrows bunched. "What the fuck are you on about?"

"Libby Nivens."

"Who?"

"Eight years old, gunned down through her own front door, at home, where she should have

228

been safe, except she wasn't, because you came along and *killed* her."

Hannah's eyes widened. "That wasn't me! Donkey did it."

George smiled, as though his patience wore thin. "I knew you'd say that. See, a witness saw it differently. The smaller of the two people fired those shots. As far as he's concerned, Donkey just stood by and watched."

Hannah pulled her lips back in a sneer. "Then he's remembering it wrong. I went round to collect a late payment, and he went off on one, got the gun out."

George smiled again, and this time it showed his disgust for her. "I'm going to find Donkey. And that gun."

Hannah laughed, although it was a little unsteady, as if she wasn't as brave as she was trying to make out. "Good luck. He's fucked off."

George strutted back and forth for a moment. "No, he hasn't. He's at home, holed up."

Hannah's expression gave her away—she wasn't sure whether to believe him or not. She was on the back foot and didn't like it. She folded her lips over her teeth, thinking. "How the fuck do *you* know?"

"It doesn't matter how I know, just that I do." George sighed — was he bored? "Are you going to get rid of that chip on your shoulder anytime soon? It's not going to change anything, acting tough, and to be honest, it's tedious."

"Why should I drop the attitude? I didn't kill that kid, and I won't take the blame for it."

If Hannah could have crossed her arms, she would have at this point. Sienna had studied her for years, watched her for signs that she'd get nasty and do something horrible to her. At the minute, Hannah was relying on her bluster to get her through. She probably thought George would believe her and set her free.

He sniffed as though she didn't too smell nice. "Did you know you were captured on a Ring doorbell? Obviously not, otherwise you wouldn't have bothered bullshitting."

"Like I'm going to believe that."

George shrugged. "Believe what you like, but the copper leading the investigation is *our* copper, and we get told all manner of things. Your car wasn't on the footage, but the witness saw it. Or should that be Sienna's car? What kind of person are you to use a relative's vehicle, knowing they'd get the blame for using it if it was caught on camera? Or was that your intention all along?"

Hannah wasn't the type to explain herself. "What witness?"

George didn't elaborate. "Shame he didn't clock the number plate, but not to worry." He bent to stare into her eyes again. "How would you like to die?"

She spat in his face. Sienna gasped; Hannah never knew when to stop.

George poked her in the cheek. "I used to think that was one of the most disgusting things someone could do to another person, it churned my stomach, but I've since realised it's done to *make* me feel that way, so I no longer give anyone the satisfaction of it upsetting me." George wiped it with his sleeve and backed away. "Answer my question."

"What does it matter how I die? Why do you want to know?"

"Because your body's going to be found by the police, and I'm curious about your thoughts on the matter. You're going to be stared at, photographed, and some people are a bit vain, aren't they, so I'm giving you the chance to pick how you're viewed."

Why was he bothering to do that? To frighten her?

Hannah displayed true fear, like she'd finally accepted this was it, the end. She shook, her bandaged hand trembling so much it knocked against the side of the seat.

"There's the shot to the head," he went on. "Indicates an execution, which is apt in this case as it shows the killer's contempt, that you were sought out, found, and murdered for killing Libby. The police will get the gist. Then there's a battered face, all those bruises, the split lip, the broken nose, an angry killer, wanting to inflict pain for what you've done. Or there's strangulation, where you'd look like you'd just fallen asleep, bar the bruising on your throat, the snapped hyoid bone—because it will snap. Or you could be stabbed, showing a frenzied, emotional attack. Up to you. Sienna doesn't mind whatever you choose."

"Sienna?" Hannah glanced from George to her. "What's *she* got to do with anything?"

"Oh, didn't I say?" George smiled. "She's your killer."

Sienna's stomach went over.

Am I?

Chapter Seventeen

This wasn't how it was supposed to go. Sienna wasn't meant to defect, to be on The Brothers' side, and neither was Two-Time. Hearing that Sienna would be her killer brought on such rage, Hannah had a hard time containing it. Livid, she was fucking livid. Abel had told her parents that baby would bring trouble, that they should have killed it and cremated it with Yvette, but they'd drawn the line at murdering a child.

Hannah hadn't. Many a time she'd had her hands around that little throat, Mum catching her the last time, barking at her to get away, and if she ever found her doing that again, she'd find herself at the clinic, and Hannah had known what that meant—she might not walk out of it.

The threat had been enough to stop her from being caught in the act but not for her to do everything she could to get the kid in trouble. When they were older, she pushed her over, punched her, kicked her, then played innocent when Sienna had run to Mum about it.

To have Sienna kill her was the ultimate insult.

Murdering Libby Nivens hadn't been in her plans last night, but the crimson lens had overtaken her, zipping her back to the past, and the shape she'd seen through the glass panels hadn't been Libby's but Sienna's. The gun had been in her hand before she'd realised it, and all she'd wanted to do was shoot her in the stomach, in the place where babies grew, telling herself she was shooting Yvette and murdering Sienna before she'd had a chance to be born. Hannah had snapped out of that fantasy pretty quickly and, knowing she couldn't let the kid live to tell tales like Sienna used to, she'd raised the gun and fired off two more shots.

She'd had a few of those episodes throughout her life, out-of-body experiences she couldn't explain. She wanted one now, where she could hover above herself, thinking about anything but what was about to happen to her. She had so many plans, to grow the business, to become a female George, inspiring fear, respect, everyone afraid of her.

It wasn't going to happen now.

Seeing him when that blindfold had come off... It had become so clear, then, that the lock-up shenanigans had been a farce. And she'd fallen for it. What had they done, forced Sienna and Two-Time to obey them?

She glared at Sienna, willing her to refuse to become a murderer, to be the wimp she really was, but her cousin eyed her back, defiance in her eyes one second, uncertainty the next. No, she'd never been a proper part of the family, didn't have the same mettle as anyone else. She'd shit herself if she had to pull a trigger. Brick it at the last minute.

"You haven't got the balls," Hannah taunted.

"You don't know me, not really," Sienna threw back. "I've behaved, done whatever I was told, but I've grown my own set of bollocks now, and they're bigger than yours."

"Whatever. You can tell yourself that all you like, but you'll always be a lily-livered bitch to me. Dad knew it, Abel knew it, but by the time I was proved right, it was too late."

Sienna inhaled deeply, as if Hannah bored her. "I'm going to make something of myself, be richer than you ever were. I'm going to run the business my way."

That got Hannah's goat, but she was impotent, couldn't do anything about it. "It doesn't belong to you. It's *my* inheritance."

"I don't give a toss. It's mine now."

Hannah smirked, testing Sienna. "Come on then, kill me. Show me those bollocks you're so proud of."

Sienna viewed Hannah with pity, and it stung. Where had she got this courage from? Surely that therapist hadn't worked her magic that quickly. And was Sienna stupid? It was so obvious, with her still roped to her chair, that she was as much in the shit as Hannah was. If she was *really* going to be allowed to kill her, George would have freed her by now.

Sienna stared ahead at George. "I'll wait for George to give me the green light, something we should have done with the business. I kept telling you we needed permission, but you were just like Dad, saying leaders needed to keep out of it. I didn't want to go behind their backs, you *made* me."

"Because *I'm* the boss of you, no one else."

"She's her own boss," George said.

"Keep out of this, you." Hannah turned her nose up at him. "You're everything that's wrong with the East End. You're no better than Ron Cardigan. Shame someone doesn't plant a bullet in *your* forehead an' all."

Ooh, she'd hit a nerve. If his face was anything to go by, he hadn't liked her bringing Ron up.

"Him being shot is a myth." George shook his head as though she was of no consequence. "And that man's name doesn't belong in this conversation. You need to get with the programme and tell me how you want to die. Time's ticking on, and I want my bed."

Rather than give him what he wanted, refusing to obey anyone's rules but her own, Hannah opened her mouth and screamed in his face.

She'd go out *her* way, defiant to the last.

Chapter Eighteen

While Hannah alternated between shouting obscenities and screeching at the ceiling, George and Greg untied Sienna and Two-Time who both went to stand in front of Hannah, arms folded, Greg behind them with his gun up, ready to shoot them if they so much as breathed wrong.

Trust, it wasn't quite there yet, but George would manipulate their loyalty, ensure they wouldn't go back on their word to behave themselves from here on out. He had an idea for Sienna when she killed Hannah, but as for Two-Time…he'd think of something.

He folded their chairs and leant them on the wall with the others. Hannah sat on the original torture chair, the wooden one, her outrage still going strong. George winced. She was getting right on his knackers, and he needed her to shut up. If she didn't, Mad George or Ruffian would arrive, and he didn't want that. This was Sienna's show.

The work phone beeped, and he checked the message.

JANINE: NO MISSING PERSON FILE.

So Yvette's disappearance hadn't been reported. It was time to get some answers from Hannah, but first, he had to warn Sienna she might be hearing things that would hurt. He gestured for her to follow him into the bathroom.

He pressed his back to the closed door. "We've got some news about the sister issue you mentioned."

She crossed her arms, probably for self-protection, to shield herself from whatever he was about to say. He felt sorry for her, having to face up to things, but in order for her to move on, she needed the truth.

"Uncle Abel was right, wasn't he," she said. "I'm not her sister."

"No, but you're cousins."

She frowned.

"Your mum had a sister. Her name was Yvette. She's on your birth certificate, but your father is blank."

"I don't... I don't understand. Hannah's always maintained that what Abel said was rubbish, so maybe she didn't know."

"That's what we're going to find out."

Sienna bit her lip. "She won't admit it even if she *does* know. She's so loyal to Mum and Dad." She paused, thinking. "God, I need to stop thinking of them like that."

"They were your parents, so it's natural. Parents don't have to be blood. It must be a relief they aren't your real ones, though."

"God, yes, but I'm so *angry*. I had my own mum and dad, so why the fuck did *they* bring me up? I needn't have lived that life."

"We've got a private investigator on it." He told her about the financials, the money still in

Yvette's bank, the fact there was no death certificate.

"Do you think she was murdered?" she asked.

"Maybe. It could have been an accident, and there was this baby who needed to be cared for. If they gave you up to social services, there'd have been an investigation as to where your mum was, it would have put the spotlight on them, so they must have chosen to bring you up as their own rather than risk losing their business. Our bloke will work out what happened."

"Their neighbours must have known I wasn't theirs. Just thinking about the logistics of it, they took a massive risk."

"They might have moved to a different area. Another housing estate. London's a fucking big place. You can get lost here easily."

She chewed the inside of her cheek, her eyes darting where her brain worked overtime. "The birth certificate I've got has Mum and Dad on it."

"It'll be a fake."

"Jesus. I don't know how to process this."

"Janet will help you. For now, channel the anger into killing Hannah."

"I don't know if I can. Kill her, I mean."

"Then Two-Time can do it. Not a problem."

He led the way back to the warehouse. Sienna stood beside Two-Time, fists clenched, her face mottled, eyes bright.

"What are *you* staring at?" Hannah snapped. "You don't have the right to even *look* at me anymore, not after this. I always said you were a mistake, you weren't one of us. You're too like Yvette, got too much good in you."

"That saves me asking my question." George glanced at her shin wound. The blood had stopped flowing and congealed around the bullet hole. He imagined taking a knife to it and gouging the bullet out, but her screams would do his head in, so he'd dig it out after she was dead. He didn't want to waste another gun, and leaving the bullet there would mean he'd have to ditch the weapon.

Sienna blinked back tears. "Why did you lie to me? Why didn't you tell the truth when Abel did?"

"Because I swore I wouldn't. I keep my promises, unlike you. I was eight when you came along, I had Mum and Dad all to myself, but it all changed when Yvette fucked up. Her stupid actions got her into trouble, and it meant you had no one. Your dad fucked off the minute he'd

243

shagged her. No one even knows who he is, just some random one-night stand, although if Yvette's to be believed, she was raped."

George felt that 'ouch'. "You've got no compassion or tact, have you?"

"Why should I? *She* ruined everything." She spat a glob of phlegm at Sienna, but it fell short and landed on the floor.

"Where is my mother?" Sienna asked. "What happened to her?"

"She's dead, that's all you need to know, and it was all her fault."

"Why did you and Abel cut me?"

"He got a taste for it, didn't he, after he'd stabbed his wife in the gut."

"Why did you carry on doing it after he'd died?"

"Because every time I used that knife, I imagined you were Yvette and I was cutting you out of her. So you didn't exist. So you never came and fucked things up. Sharing my bedroom, eating our food, taking up all the attention."

George tutted. "This is like a bad police drama, the confession. Are we done yet?"

Hannah glared at him. "She asked me questions, I answered them, so don't blame me for the drama shit."

He looked at Sienna. Raised his eyebrows.

It seemed she'd come to a decision. "Shoot her like she shot Libby, and stab her stomach like she... Just make a mess of her." She walked, head down, towards the bathroom.

Hannah barked out a triumphant laugh. "See? I knew you couldn't do it. You're weak, like your mother."

Sienna stopped. "No, I just don't want to waste any more of my energy on a piece of shit like you."

Hannah's eyelid flickered in an almost-not-there wince. Sienna's words had hit a sore spot, and George smiled. Sienna went into the bathroom, and he hoped she could control her emotions enough not to cry loudly, to give Hannah satisfaction.

George stooped to take her shoes off. He went to the table, selected a cigar cutter, and crouched in front of her, his next act just for shits and giggles. Two quick snips, and she no longer owned little toes. Instead of screaming, she panted, groans and exhalations seeping through the gaps in her clenched teeth. He strode away from her, dropping the cutter in a bucket of bleach water, then checked Two-Time to see how he coped with all this.

The bloke didn't seem fazed.

Good.

George stood in front of Hannah. "Where's the body?" He kicked her shin wound.

Hannah roared out a scream, tears streaming. She raised her knees, then pointed her toes to the floor, pressing down, the ends going white, the nails blanching. It took a couple of minutes for her to calm down.

"I don't know. The clinic got rid of it."

"What clinic?"

"The one I went to today."

"What's it called?"

She told him, and George's anger level rose. It was the same clinic Moon used. Christ, he wasn't going to be happy a body had been disposed of on his patch, unless he knew about Yvette back in the day and had agreed to it.

"That's good," he said. "We'll find out what happened to her."

"I doubt it. The man who dealt with it is dead."

"So? You think that'll stop us?" George put on a face mask and pulled his hood up, leaving only his eyes visible. The perfect disguise. He looked at Greg. "Video this, will you?"

Greg got his phone out.

"What's going on?" Hannah said. "Get that fucking camera away from me."

George punched her in the stomach, the ropes around it taking the brunt. In his Scottish accent, he said, "Not everything's about you." He smiled at Two-Time. "You can kill her, and the film is our insurance."

Two-Time shrugged. "Fine by me."

"Knives are on the table."

Two-Time wandered over there, choosing the longest blade. George went behind Hannah and loosened the knot, unravelling the rope enough so her stomach was on view but she was still secured to the chair. He tugged her hands out, interested to see her trying to defend herself and getting nowhere. A bit of amusement for him. He tied it back up then held her shoulders so she couldn't stand.

Two-Time came round the front, the knife in his fist. "I'm going to enjoy this."

He shoved her T-shirt up, tucked it into her bra. Plunged the blade into her gut. She didn't scream, not at first, the shock of it rendering her speechless, then an animalistic wail came out of her wide-open mouth, her hands flailing, reaching up to try to grab George. He crouched, slid his hands down to her wrists, and pulled, hard, hoping he tore ligaments and tendons. The chair jolted from another stab, then another, and the stench of fresh piss came a second before urine slapped on the floor. George watched it drip into a puddle, the chair jostling again. Eight times, all told, and he guessed there was one for every year of Libby's life.

Two-Time was a man after his own heart.

George let her wrists go and stood. Peered over her at the mess. Two strips in amongst it, ribbons, tagliatelle, and he laughed, eyeing up the blood and gore that poked between them. He bent and shouted in her ear, "I bet that hurt, just like it hurt Sienna."

"Fuck you," she blasted out. "Fuck. You."

She gasped, staring at her stomach, slapping her hands on it in an attempt to stem the blood flow which oozed into the hand bandage. There was too much, thick and viscous and spreading.

George drew the zip of his white suit down and ferreted for his gun, passing it to Two-Time over Hannah's bowed head. The bloke took it, cocked the safety, curled his finger around the trigger. George gripped her short hair at the side, yanking her head up, and moved out of range.

"If you miss and I get shot..." George smiled. "Wouldn't advise it."

Two-Time aimed. Fired. George took his hand off her hair in the same millisecond the bullet struck. The back of her head burst open, the bullet embedding in the wall above the table. Brain matter slapped on the floor, a fine mist of blood suspended then falling. She propelled backwards from the blast, the chair crashing to the concrete.

George held his hand out for the gun. Two-Time passed it over, his attention still on Hannah, who stared, her eyes blank, her life gone, just like that.

No more cutting, bullying, killing.

Greg put the phone away.

"You belong to us now," George said, his East End brogue back now the camera had stopped rolling.

Two-Time nodded. "Good."

Chapter Nineteen

S*adie had grown older, although she wasn't Sadie anymore but Sienna, a stupid name in Hannah's opinion. It had turned out like Uncle Abel had predicted: Auntie Yvette dying, the baby coming to live with them. Not only that, but they'd had to move house, Hannah going to a new school, and she'd been sworn to secrecy, told to tell everyone Sienna was her sister, not her cousin. It had been a lot for Hannah to*

deal with at eight years old, and the crimson lens had come often during that uncertain time.

Mum and Dad were out on a rare date night, and it was Hannah's responsibility to watch Sienna, what with her being older. As a teen, Hannah struggled not only with her strange and violent thoughts but with hormones, too, and she fancied girls, not boys, which was confusing and against everything Dad had taught her.

"Lesbians only belong in porn for men's enjoyment, all tarted up and pretty," he'd said, "and none of them should look like men. All those birds with short hair, bloody nasty dykes."

Hannah wanted to cut her hair, but his words had put her off. He'd call her a dyke if she did, and she couldn't handle his brand of ridicule, how nonprogressive he was. He was a cruel man at his core, she'd come to realise that, and maybe that's why she was cruel in her thoughts and visions. Was it hereditary? Had his spite been passed down to her? Did he have secret fantasies where he killed people with machetes?

She flopped down on the sofa, watching yet another Disney princess film. Sienna loved them, and rather than go through the rigmarole of telling her they needed to take it in turns, Hannah just let her have her own way. It was something she'd noticed Mum did, too. It was as if Sienna being here was a hassle and if they could make their lives nicer by doing 'anything for a quiet life', then that's what they'd do.

Mum was resentful about taking Sienna on, it had been obvious from the start. She hadn't liked having to get up in the night to feed a baby, to keep to herself a lot because she didn't want to invite questions, especially not from any health visitors, who were apparently a nosy bunch. Sienna hadn't been taken to a local doctor, ever, all of her jabs and whatever were done at the private clinic, something Mum begrudged paying for. Hannah could see her point. Because of Auntie Yvette dying, Mum's life had changed the most out of all of them.

Dad had made no bones about Sienna being an inconvenience at first. She was that all right, and Hannah couldn't stand the little bitch. They didn't even look like sisters, their hair different colours, their features so obviously not those of siblings. You'd think there'd be some resemblance, what with them being cousins, but no. Someone had remarked once that Mum must have been seeing the milkman. At the time, Hannah hadn't understood what that had meant, but she had a good idea now.

If only they knew…

"This is so crap," Hannah muttered.

Sienna looked over at Hannah, her expression giving away her hurt. "You're a meanie head."

"Whatever. Once this is finished, you're going to bed."

"Mum said I can stay up until ten cos it's a Saturday."

"But Mum's not here, and it's me looking after you, not her."

Sienna's eyes filled with tears, and she turned to the telly, her bottom lip sticking out. Hannah watched her. Had she ever been annoying like that? Had she sulked when she hadn't got her own way? She didn't think she had, she'd been too concerned with trying to act normal, to hide who she really was inside.

The doorbell rang, and as their pizza had already been delivered, Hannah frowned and got up. In the hallway, she peered through the spyhole. Uncle Abel stood on the path, hands in pockets, a beanie hat pulled low. She opened up and stepped back.

"What are you doing here?" she asked.

"It's time." He locked them in and hung his coat on the row of hooks.

"Time for what?"

"Don't you remember what we talked about?" he said, his voice low. "About her belly?"

Of course she remembered, she'd thought about it every single day since that night, had envisaged it before she fell asleep, but it wasn't a good idea, not anymore. "She's going to tell on us. She's not the sort to keep it quiet. You know how she is. The minute I do anything to her, she runs off to Mum."

Hannah picked on Sienna as often as she could, sticking her foot out to trip her, barging into her so she thumped into a wall or fell over. Pinching her. Poking her in the back. It was the only way she could control her other urges, ones involving machetes.

"Don't you worry about that," *Abel whispered,* "she'll soon understand who's boss. That kid needs taking down a peg. She rules you all."

"But Mum's going to see the cuts. She sits on the toilet lid while Sienna has a bath."

"Still? Well, it's about time Sienna had a bath on her own, then, isn't it."

"What if you cut too deep and she needs to go to the hospital?"

Abel glowered at her. "Are you denying me my pleasure? I've waited a fucking long time to do this, and it seems you're trying to stop me. You can still be put into care, you know."

"For what?"

His sinister smile chilled her.

"Teenage delinquent. I can fit you up for all sorts." He folded his arms.

She'd underestimated him. Yes, she knew full well what he did for Mum and Dad, how wicked he was to people who didn't pay up in time, but she'd stupidly thought he cared about her, like a real uncle. No, all he cared about was hurting Sienna, or whoever else he cut, and if Hannah stood in his way, he'd make sure she was dealt with.

The realisation stung.

"Why do you even need me anyway?" she asked.

"To hold her down."

She deflated a bit. Thought he'd let her have a go at using the knife. "Oh."

"Come on. Watch and learn, kid."

The evening had turned into one so bizarre, Hannah had to pinch herself to check if it was real. The way Abel had spoken to Sienna, how he'd frightened her into doing whatever he'd said so quickly, was a masterclass in coercion. At no point had Sienna said she'd tell Mum and Dad, she'd just obeyed, scared out of her mind about being taken away and put into a home. Hannah was scared about the same thing if she didn't comply in aiding and abetting.

The cuts had been shallow, the blood minimal, and by tomorrow, they'd be long, thin scabs, similar to Hannah scratching her skin whenever she had the crimson visions, her attempt at clawing out whatever lived inside her. The badness. That evil, dark passenger, although she had no idea how she'd feel without it. It belonged to her, was her, and she couldn't imagine not hearing that growly voice telling her what to do if people pissed her off. She'd read enough to know she was mentally ill, but as before, she couldn't tell her parents. They wouldn't understand, but Abel did.

They whispered in the hallway afterwards, Sienna tucked up in bed.

"You're like me," he said. "Carrying something wicked around with you. Why do you think I need to cut? To hurt? If I don't, I'd be screwed up, I can tell you."

He'd been so casual, as if he'd come to terms with who he was, every part of him, and it was natural to take his fantasies out on innocent people. How much had his wife suffered before she'd killed herself? How much would Sienna suffer now, and for how long?

Why had he chosen her? Did he have others he tormented, too?

"You're screwed up anyway for even doing it," she muttered, then, seeing his dark look, added, "But I get it. I feel so much better after that."

"Did you like holding her down?"

"Yeah."

"Made you feel powerful, didn't it?"

"Yeah."

"Wait until you get your chance to cut her. You'll feel invincible then."

"When's it my turn?"

"Not for a good while yet. You need to learn how much pressure to apply. You need to watch me for a while longer."

Worry nagged at her. "What if she isn't as scared as we thought and she tells on us?"

"Then we'll deny it. It'll look like she's done it to herself. I had a little word when I put her to bed—and just happened to hide one of your mum's knives under it. They'll automatically blame her when they see it."

She got up the courage to ask, "Are you a paedo or something? Like, because you picked a little girl?"

"Don't be so disgusting."

But he looked guilty, and she shuddered at the thought of him thinking about her and Sienna like that.

"She's an easy target, same as you," he said. "Nothing more. Women, unless I've been in a relationship with them for a while and I've controlled them, they tend to have more about them where they'd go to the police. You two… Nah. Sienna will put up with it, and you will, too, because admit it, you enjoyed it. I saw it in your eyes. You hate her, and hurting her makes you feel better."

She couldn't deny it, and once he'd left, she stood at her bedroom window, waiting for the sound of Dad's key going in the lock and her parents laughing because they'd drunk too much on their date. She worried Sienna would blurt it out in the morning, or have a nightmare and go into Mum and Dad's room, saying Abel and Hannah had been nasty to her.

That night, Hannah didn't sleep. She went over the scenario again and again, putting herself in Abel's place, and later, no Abel at all, Hannah the only one to administer the cuts. And they were deep, so deep they needed stitches, which she sewed, Sienna screaming from the pain of the needle jabbing into her.

One day, that would happen. One day, she'd have Sienna so far under her thumb, her 'sister' would do whatever she wanted.

Hannah smiled at the thought.

It had become a regular thing. Once a month, on date nights, Abel turned up, and Hannah pinned Sienna down on the living room floor while he did the cutting. Sienna had done as she'd been instructed and told Mum she wanted to have a bath alone now. She'd changed, no longer the spoilt little cow but withdrawn, so much so that Mum had just commented on it.

"Are you being bullied?" she asked as they sat around the table, eating.

It was Tuesday, so it was dinner from the chippy.

Mum and Sienna sat opposite Hannah and Dad.

Dad harrumphed. "The best way to deal with bullies it to hit them back when they least expect it."

"That's not how it works these days," Mum said. "The school don't allow that sort of thing to go on anymore."

"Get them after school, then," Dad said. "All these new rules do my head in. Back in our day, you just lumped someone and told them to fuck off."

"Well, it isn't our day, is it, it's theirs." Mum poured mushy peas out of the polystyrene container onto her chips. "New rules." She raised her eyebrows at Sienna. "Well, are you being bullied?"

Hannah speared a piece of battered sausage and gave Sienna 'the look'. Sienna's cheeks turned red, and she was on the verge of tears. Hannah kicked her under the table, for a moment thinking she'd hit the wrong leg and it was Mum's.

"No," Sienna said.

"Something's wrong, because you don't laugh anymore." Mum sipped from her can of Coke.

Sienna shrugged.

"I'm not going to push you," Mum went on. "I really can't be arsed."

Sienna hung her head and ate a chip.

That had been tense. Hannah had worried Sienna would blab, but then again, with the threat from Abel last week, that he'd break in at night and stab her to death in her bed, well, it was no wonder she hadn't spilled the beans.

A spread of warmth went through Hannah. Being in control like this, Abel's little helper, the one who watched Sienna for signs that she'd break down and confess what was going on, gave her such a sense of importance she couldn't stop herself from smiling.

"What's tickled you?" Mum asked.

"Just something Laura said at school today. Nothing special."

The meal continued as usual, Dad saying they needed to get a move on if they were going to meet the new client on time. Hannah was on babysitting duty again, and she couldn't wait to torment Sienna about the upcoming Saturday night. By the time she was finished, her stupid sister would be in tears, gulping between sobs, and promising that she'd never tell a soul—about any of it.

Like a good girl.

Sienna hated everyone around the table, even Mum. She didn't belong here with these people, she realised that now. That first night, after...after Abel had cut her, he'd taken her to bed and told her she was an 'interloper'. She didn't know what that meant and wasn't sure she wanted to. It was bound to be something horrible.

He came while Mum and Dad were out. Held down on the floor by her sister, Sienna always prayed they'd come home early, catch them at it. She wouldn't get the blame for telling tales then, they'd see it all for *themselves. Mum hadn't even noticed the blood on Sienna's vests when she did the washing, and Sienna reckoned Hannah snatched them away and cleaned them.*

Why was Hannah so mean? Why did she let Uncle Abel cut her? Why were they even doing it? But she knew why, Abel had told her. As the interloper, she could be treated any way they chose. She had to 'pay the price for coming into our lives'. Suffer for the sins of her mother.

That didn't make sense.

What had Mum done for Sienna to be treated this way?

Chapter Twenty

George left it to Greg to drop Sienna and Two-Time home. George's idea of taking a photo of Sienna standing next to Hannah's body, a gun in her hand, was a good move. Now they had insurance on both of them, and George had the shin bullet in his pocket, wrapped in tissue, so if she ever stepped out of line, he'd plant it in her flat and ring Janine. He'd told Sienna that, put the wind right up her, and she'd reiterated again that she wouldn't be telling anyone about this, she just wanted to move on. Forget it all. Look like Alice, whatever the fuck that meant.

Dwayne had brought a stolen car to the warehouse, the plates changed, and Hannah was currently stuffed in the boot, her shoes with her. George had his Ruffian disguise on, a clean forensic suit covering his clothes, and the crew would get the warehouse shipshape while the rest of London slept.

It was one a.m., and he'd driven through the streets, avoiding cameras as much as possible, but it didn't matter if the car was spotted when the police got stuck into the new investigation. He planned to torch it at the scene and walk home, and his beard and whatever were enough to hide his identity.

He turned down the track that led into Daffodil Woods, the place some of the dead refugee women had been found in the spring. The police had scoured every inch of it, looking for more victims, but no others had been discovered there. It felt a bit obscene to be here, in light of what had gone on back then, but the woods veered off with other tracks, like the branches of a tree, easy for him to navigate, easy for him to hide the car while he posed the body.

Janine would have his guts for garters when she saw it, and he smiled, parking behind a stand of pines. He took Hannah from the boot, carried her over to a nearby oak, and got to work.

Chapter Twenty-One

Janine answered her work phone, glad to see an unknown number on her screen. George would do his usual and throw the SIM away, but she still endured a streak of anxiety zipping through her stomach at him forgetting, the phone location being tracked to his address. She didn't want him caught. Much as he was a monster sometimes and should be behind bars, she couldn't help but like the bastard.

"It's me," George said.

She tutted. "I gathered that."

"I'll keep it short and sweet. Daffodil Woods. Tarra."

She'd opened her mouth to ask the specific location, but he'd ended the call. "Fucking twat."

She got out of bed and phoned it in, giving them the unknown number so they could go through the motions, then she rang Colin.

"Boss?"

"Sorry, we've got a shout."

"Bloody hell," he said, sleepy, a yawn chasing the words away. "Can you pick me up? Suzie's on nights and has the car."

"Yep, I'll be with you in half an hour. I need to shower and whatever, and the station's organising first responders, so I'm not rushing."

She had a shower, made coffee in to-go cups, locked her place up, and drove to Colin's a few streets away. She was playing it by the book, didn't fancy turning up at Daffodil by herself. She'd done that before when George had left a body for her, but it hadn't been in such a creepy place. She'd been rapped over the knuckles for not following protocol, so this time, she'd be good.

Colin staggered from his semi-detached, blundered down his path, and flumped into the passenger seat. He dragged his seat belt across as if it weighed a ton. "Fucking hell, retirement can't come soon enough."

"How many times have you said that since being on my team? I agree, though, it's shit when you've got to hang around for the pension." She pulled away from the kerb.

"Tell me about it."

"There's a coffee for you in the cup holder. Only instant, I'm afraid."

"You bloody lifesaver. I don't give a shit what it is so long as it wets my whistle." He took one out, eyed the steam coming from the cut-out hole, and grumbled, "That's going to burn, isn't it."

"Take the sodding lid off then and blow it."

He did, not yet brave enough to take the first sip. "Where are we going?"

"Daffodil Woods."

"Christ, not another refugee?"

"No. It's apparently Libby's killer."

He jolted in shock, spilling some coffee on his black trousers. "Shit, shit." He rubbed it in.

"That'll leave a red mark now. And how the fuck do you know it's to do with Libby?"

"Anonymous call to my work phone."

"How did they get your number?"

"I've given out countless business cards over the years, so they could have got it from that. Don't forget, people can find anything out if they try hard enough." She wished she hadn't said that last part. It gave her shivers to think *she* might be found out eventually.

"What did they say?"

"That they'd killed her and dumped her in the woods, ending with: Justice for Libby." She'd just lied, but whatever.

"Not too dramatic, then." He rolled his eyes and blew his drink again.

"They sounded pretty pleased with themselves, I have to say."

"Man or a woman?"

"A bloke."

"I wonder if it's the fella who was with her on the doorstep."

"I thought the same. Maybe she told him she'd get him in the shit for it, and he flipped. He might not have known she was going to kill the girl and they rowed about it. Who bloody knows."

She left him to ponder whatever a hate-my-job copper pondered and continued driving in silence. By the time they arrived, she'd thrown out all thoughts of George cocking up somehow, leaving a part of himself behind. She shoved herself into detective mode, as if she didn't already know who'd killed Hannah Weggley.

"What's that?" Colin asked, pointing out of the window.

Janine studied the sky. A grey, cloud-like puff rose in a deeper part of the woods.

If George has set fire to her… "Looks like smoke to me."

"A charred body. Just what we don't need."

A cordon had been set up at the mouth of the main track, a uniform standing guard. The SOCO van had arrived—the first responders must have already found the body, then—and officers stood at the rear, putting suits on. She parked at the verge behind a patrol car and sipped her coffee. The scene manager's car was also here, so Sheila Sutton was probably off investigating the source of the smoke. Either the cogs had turned quickly while Janine had been getting ready or she'd been longer than she'd thought in getting ready.

"This could take all night," Colin grumped.

"Which is why we'll finish our coffees before we get out. How's Suzie?"

"Full of the joys of spring. She leaves work next week."

"Sucks to be you, having to stay on for another, what, five years?"

"You know damn well how long it is. Stop winding me up."

She smiled. "Don't worry, I'll be kind to you and don't expect you to pull your weight. I prefer bearing the brunt anyway. You can just tag along and get paid for it."

"I appreciate that."

And I appreciate that you're happy to keep out of my business. "Maybe someone will do the same for me when I'm your age."

He stared through the windscreen. "Jim will be happy if a body's found and it turns out to be Libby's killer."

"We all will. It's affected everyone really badly. How was he during the post-mortem?"

"I swear he was crying at one point. He wiped his face with his sleeve."

"Poor sod."

Colin finished his drink and popped the cup in the holder. "What do you think about the father?"

"He's hiding something."

"Hmm."

Coffee gone, the SOCO officers all dressed up, Janine reckoned they ought to make a move, especially now Sheila Sutton came from somewhere farther along the track, waving both hands in the air, her usual signal that she needed a tent.

"She's definitely got a body," Janine said. "Come on."

They grabbed protectives from the back of the van, signed the log, and followed SOCO down the track. One carried lights, and two others hefted a tent between them. Janine overtook them, following Sheila's call, turning onto a left-hand fork. Orange flickers undulated between the tree trunks in the distance. George had either burnt the body for some strange, infuriating reason, or he'd torched the vehicle he'd used to bring it here.

The latter became apparent as she skirted round a cluster of pines and ended up in a clearing. A SOCO streaked past, carrying a fire extinguisher, which wouldn't do anything but put the already-dying flames out. Going by the state of the car, any evidence was long gone. The windows had burst out, the interior blackened, and the officer aimed the stream inside it to put out what was left of the fire.

"Blimey," Colin said, catching up, out of breath. "Someone wanted to cover their tracks."

Janine left him gawping, moving over to Sheila and two uniforms, where they stood by a magnificent oak, its trunk wide. Their torchlights pointed at the victim, although Janine wouldn't think of Hannah as that now. She was scum.

A woman sat against it, a very dead woman, a bullet hole in her forehead, her T-shirt tucked into her bra. Knife wounds had wrecked her stomach, and a bloodied bandage covered one hand.

From where George shot her finger off.

A large patch of blood surrounded a slit in her jeans at the shin, as if it had been sliced with a sharp knife, revealing what was an obvious bullet wound—the bone had a hole in it—the flesh hacked at.

George removing the bullet?

She didn't have any little toes, so Janine surmised she'd been tortured, although from what she could see, George hadn't beaten her up. No bruising. She glanced around for shoes, couldn't see any, so guessed they were in the car. The SOCO with the lights set them up, and the area flooded bright, the blood so much starker now, the damage to the body clearer.

"I heard you got an anon call," Sheila said.

"Yes. They claim to have killed the woman who murdered Libby Nivens."

"Can't say I've got any sympathy for her, then." She gestured to the body. "But what a way to go."

"She deserves all she got," one of the uniforms muttered.

Janine didn't disagree. "No weapons around?"

"Not yet." Sheila sighed. "I'll ring Jim."

The grumpy uniformed officer stepped away, shaking his head, and the photographer took his place. Everyone moved back to let SOCO get on with the tent. Janine followed Sheila who checked the ground as she walked, heading for some bushes.

"I doubt we'll get lucky and find the gun she used on Libby," Sheila said.

Janine thought otherwise. If George had found it, it would be here. "There might still be gunshot residue on her, though. That could be enough."

"We live in hope."

Janine needed to get hold of George and find out where that gun was. If he'd left it in the car, she'd verbally rip him a new one. "I'll just have a wander round, see if her accomplice has been dumped, too."

"Okay."

Janine walked down yet another track, going far enough that the light from her burner phone wouldn't be seen with her back to the main scene. She took it out and tapped in a message, a response coming quickly.

GG: IT ISN'T AT HER FLAT. I HAD PEOPLE THERE LOOKING FOR IT WHILE SHE WAS BEING DEALT WITH. I ASSUME THE FELLA'S GOT IT OR IT WAS DUMPED. IF WE DO GET OUR HANDS ON IT, YOU'LL BE THE FIRST TO KNOW.

JANINE: OKAY. WHAT'S HAPPENING ABOUT HIM?

GG: MARTIN'S KEEPING WATCH OUTSIDE HIS PLACE. WE'LL BE PAYING HIM A VISIT ABOUT SIX A.M. NEED A BIT OF KIP FIRST.

JANINE: CAN'T YOU JUST GO AND GET HIM NOW?

GG: KNOB OFF, I'M KNACKERED.

She gritted her teeth, deleted the messages, and slid the phone away.

"Got anything?" Colin asked from behind her.

She resisted jumping a mile. Why had he crept up on her? "The caller didn't say he'd killed two people, but I'm looking anyway. What are you doing here? I thought you wanted to stay out of things as much as possible."

"I do, but the victim's got some strips of skin in her mouth."

"Um, what?"

"Yeah, they look a bit dried out and don't match any of the cuts on her belly. Like, they're not from her stomach."

"Is Jim here already, then?"

"No."

"So who's got close enough to the body to see that?"

"One of the uniforms was talking to the other about it. I was earwigging."

"Fuck it. We'll have to go back."

Colin sighed. "Balls, I came to help you so I didn't have to hear anything else."

"You have a mooch around instead of me, then. I'll deal with it."

"Cheers, boss."

She wanted to message George again, but almost getting caught by Colin had set her nerves alight. She returned to the scene, approached the body, and crouched. Hannah's mouth hung open, and the skin was farther in. A good spot by the uniform, because Janine hadn't seen it the first time round.

She stood. "Any ID as to who she is?"

No one answered.

She'd have to wait for Jim. He'd go spare if anyone poked in Hannah's pockets for a purse. She stared at the woman again, bent over, and cocked her head to peer into the mouth.

What the fuck are you playing at, George?

Chapter Twenty-Two

The twins arrived outside Donkey's house, George waving at Martin for him to go home since he'd sat in a car all night, keeping watch. The place was an obvious one-bedroom effort, slim, no front garden, and old. The brickwork needed cleaning, so filthy it bordered on black rather than the red it had once been, the windows likely letting in the cold during the winter, the frames were that rickety. Still, as it butted to the pavement, it would make it easier to bundle Donkey into the back of the van, less chance of them being spotted.

It was six a.m. on the dot, but regardless, some bloke down the road got into his car and drove off. Grabbing the opportunity, before someone else left their home, George gave Greg the nod, and they both got out, disguised in their forensic suits, beards, and glasses, hoods up.

Greg approached the door and got on with picking the lock, opening the door a crack. George breathed a sigh of relief that a chain hadn't been slid into place. Greg stuffed the pick into a pocket, opened the door wider, and took his gun out, holding it up. He entered, swirling one hand in the air for George to follow. Greg checked the room on the left then walked up the hallway into the kitchen, light from the early morning sun splashing on the mixer tap at the sink directly ahead.

George stepped inside, closed the door to, and opted for the stairs. He went slowly, mindful they might creak, but made it to the top with no surprise noises. On the square of landing, he peered into a small bathroom in front of him, then moved right to what could only be the bedroom door.

It stood ajar, so he leant forward to peer through the gap. Short, thin curtains allowed light to come through, a white chest of drawers under them, the middle drawer open, a jumble of clothes spilling out. He eased the door forward in increments, gun in hand, poking his head round. The bed was at the other end, beneath the front window, the quilt thrown off, Donkey sprawled on his back, legs spread, knackers on show. George had the urge to put a bullet in them but refrained. He inched the door to its full extent. Paused, listening to the man's steady breathing. It was too deep for him to be pretending to sleep. The nearby fan provided a steady hum.

George stalked forward, his steps slow. At the side of the bed, he trained the gun on Donkey, then, careful as you like, got on the bed, holding his breath in anticipation of the bloke waking up. George cocked his leg then settled into a straddling position, bending over so his face was close, their noses almost touching. He pressed the end of the gun to Donkey's temple.

The fella's eyes opened, languid, as if he'd either drunk a skinful the night before or he'd smoked a shedload of weed. It didn't seem to register at first that a man sat on him, and his eyebrows bunched, his brain taking a while to fire up.

"Morning, my old son."

Donkey's eyes widened, and he automatically made a move to bolt upright, realisation kicking in fully now. He relaxed, stared up at George, then his eyes swung to one side, to where the gun was.

"I wouldn't advise trying anything," George said. "My trigger finger might get a bit happy, know what I mean?"

A quick nod.

"Now then, sources tell me you were with Hannah when Libby Nivens got shot. Nasty business, that, killing a kid. Hannah's dead, and now it's your turn."

The shuffle of movement from behind, then, "What the fuck are you doing, bruv?"

George smiled. "Always wanted to sit on a donkey."

Greg tutted. "Fuck's sake. Stop pratting about and get off him. We need to make a move."

George sat upright. "Did you hear that, sunshine? We're going for a little ride."

Naked, Donkey sat roped to the wooden chair in the warehouse, wide awake, the shock of his situation sinking in. Greg had removed his outfit and disguise, revealing he was one half of a duo Donkey really didn't want to tangle with, but it was too late for regrets. George wasn't interested in any sob stories, although he did want to know exactly how things had gone down on the night of Libby's murder so he could pass it on to Janine.

He paced in front of the man, smacking his cricket stump on his gloved palm. He had no intention of using it, just liked the slapping sound and how it sent people a bit doo-lally, frightening them, all manner of questions zipping through their minds: *What's he going to do with that? Is that dried blood on the end?*

George had opened new tools for this job, he didn't want any cross-contamination going on. He'd had his fill of creating ribbons on Pete, although he still had a couple of strips he'd stuff in Donkey's mouth when he dumped the body. Janine would be cursing him, wondering why he'd done it to Hannah, but this job had all started with Pete, and the link to him had seemed poignant at the time. Besides, it would be what the coppers would call his MO for this double murder, and he quite liked the idea of them trying to work out who the skin belonged to.

"So," he said, "what the fuck went on that night?"

"I swear, I didn't know she had a gun on her. Didn't even know she intended to kill anyone. We were just supposed to go there, put the shits up Nivens for a laugh, then leave."

"Except it didn't go that way, did it."

"No. Hannah was guffing on about the kid going to get her dad, but the girl wouldn't do it. I think Hannah went into some sort of rage inside her head, because she wouldn't listen to me when I told her to leave it. Like she had this red mist she couldn't see past."

George knew that feeling. "Why didn't you go back to the car and leave her to it?"

"Because the mood she was in, she'd have shot me."

"Did she get into those moods a lot, then?"

"Yeah, every now and then she loses the plot. Sees herself as a gangster. Someone nobody can touch."

"Not even a big lump like you?"

"You don't know her. She's off her rocker. Proper mad. I feel sorry for Sienna the most. She's controlled, too scared to do anything against her."

"She's not scared anymore, but are you?"

Donkey laughed wryly. "Wouldn't you be if one of The Brothers stood in front of you with a cricket stump?"

"I'd have thought me sitting on you in bed with a gun to your bonce would have been scarier, but what do I know. Each to their own."

"What are you going to do?"

"Isn't it obvious?"

"Shit."

"Hmm. But we haven't finished talking yet. Hannah shot Libby, then what?"

"We nipped in the Seven Bells for a bit, then went clubbing."

"Excuse me?" That pissed George off. A little one had been gunned down, and they'd gone off to get shitfaced and had a bit of a *dance*?

Donkey grimaced. "I know, fucking rotten, but she was in one of those rages, and I couldn't say no. Plus she still had the gun on her. Said she'd shoot my brains out if I didn't go with her."

"At what point was the gun in your possession?"

"Later, when we parted ways."

"What club did you go to?"

"The Roxy."

George stopped pacing, closing his eyes momentarily. The Roxy was down the road from The Angel, and the thought of Hannah enjoying herself on such a prominent part of their patch after what she'd done got right on his nellies. Having *fun* after she'd gunned down a child.

"Why didn't you go to the police?"

Donkey's bottom lip quivered. "I thought about it. Couldn't bloody sleep when I got home."

"But...?"

"But I'd done something for her in the past, helped kill old Robertson, and she still had the knife I used. My fingerprints are on the handle."

"Oh dear. A bit like you keeping the gun *she* used. Does it have her prints on it?"

"Yeah."

Greg had found it in a box of cereal at Donkey's place, inside a plastic sandwich bag.

"Good." George pondered how he'd kill this piece of shit. While he believed the man felt remorse, he was still a penis for not dobbing Hannah in. "You could have got hold of us two instead of going to the police. We'd have found the knife, covered up for you."

"*I* didn't know that, *did* I? I've been working for her without your permission, so I thought you'd have fucked me over."

"Depends how you'd have stated your case. Anyway, it's a moot point, because you're fucked now. No going back. Who's old Robertson?"

"Some bloke who was late paying up. Hannah wanted to make a point so others would think twice about trying to shaft her. Me and Two-Time got rid of the body."

George would ask their latest recruit about that.

He walked over to the table and picked up the gun he'd used on Hannah. He returned to stand in front of Donkey. "Got any last requests?"

Donkey's eyes watered. "Fuck, this is it, isn't it?"

"Yep."

"Just...just tell my mum I'm sorry and I love her."

George refused to allow himself to feel bad for this prick, although it was tough pushing his emotions down. Those words were what he'd have wanted passed on to his own mother had he found himself in this situation. An apology for being such a disappointment, for turning out the way he had, for all the pain she'd have endured with him dead.

"We'll send her a note and a few quid to help bury you." That was all he was prepared to do.

He raised the gun, aimed it at the forehead, and pulled the trigger.

Sorted.

George couldn't go to Daffodil Woods, obviously, so he chose the next one along, coming from the other side to where the police would still be, feeling like Denny Rawlings must have when he'd picked locations to leave the dead refugees. Once again in a stolen car, a forensic suit and gloves on, he parked between two firs and took Donkey out of the boot. He was too heavy to drape over his shoulder, so he dragged him into a spot in front of the car and positioned him against the trunk of another fir, the lowest branches offering the body some shade.

How long will it be before flies congregate on his forehead?

George crouched and put the ribbons of skin in Donkey's mouth, then placed the gun, still in the sandwich bag, beside the bloke's thigh. He backed out from the canopy and got on with torching the car. It caught quickly, so he ran through the woods and out the opposite side, where Greg waited for him in the work van, today's logo on the side panel a mop and bucket and the words: THE CARDIGAN ESTATE CLEANER, NO JOB TOO SMALL!

George buckled up and opened the glove compartment, taking out a lemon sherbet. "Do you want one?"

"No." Greg drove away. "That smoke's a dead giveaway."

"Yep." George shoved the sweet in his mouth, tucking it against his cheek. He lifted a new burner from the centre console and jabbed in Janine's number.

She answered but didn't speak.

"Can you talk?" he asked. "Or at least listen?"

"Hmm."

He took it that she wasn't in a position to have an in-depth chat, which suited him because she

291

couldn't chew his ear off about the ribbons in Hannah's mouth. "Snowdrop Woods. Gun found. I left it there. It has her prints on it."

"Who are you?" she said, likely because someone was earwigging or watching.

"Joe Bloggs." He laughed, cut the call, and removed the SIM. Threw it out of the window into a hedgerow. "I suppose we should give her a pay rise really."

Greg shrugged. "She earns a fair whack off us as it is, and think of all the times she doesn't even have to do anything yet still gets paid."

"True. She can have a bonus then, seeing as I left that skin and she'll have extra on her plate chasing that up."

"What?"

"I put those bits of Pete's skin in their gobs."

"*What*?"

Greg turned right into the breaker's yard. George could get his suit off soon, and the fella who owned it could valet the van using certain chemicals to get rid of any evidence.

George sighed. "You heard me."

"I did, but what I meant to say was, are you out of your mind? What the fuck was the point in doing that?"

"Dunno, seemed the right thing to do."

"It's sick, sicker than your usual behaviour. Like, serial killer sick. You need to get yourself another therapist, mate."

George laughed. "D'you reckon Janet will recommend one?"

Greg laughed, too, shaking his head, and he parked round the back of a pile of broken vehicles that waited to be crushed. "Seriously, though, you need to stop these weird little things you're doing. Now the police are going to have to look into who the skin belongs to. What if they've got a record of Pete's DNA?"

"So what if they have?"

"It means them poking into shit, finding out Pete's gone missing, and they'll go round to Zoe and Genevieve to see if they've seen him, heard from him."

George realised his mistake, although it was too fucking late to rectify it now. What was it he'd said to Genevieve? That they couldn't risk the police going round there and, for whatever reason, getting forensics in, finding his blood no matter how much she'd bleached the place.

"Bollocks," he said and could see Greg's point about a new therapist. "I can't trust anyone but Janet, though."

"Then go and see her. Fuck whether you were an item, you need to get that impulsive part of your brain sorted out, because shit like the stunt you've just pulled could come back to bite us on the arse one day."

"Sorry."

"So you fucking should be." Greg got out and headed for the portacabin office.

George stripped his outfit off then did the same, nodding to their contact who knew the drill—burn the clothes, clean the van, switch the number plates, strip the decals off. In the portacabin, George sat at the staff table while Greg boiled the kettle and busied himself with making them a cuppa.

George felt bad. "I'll phone Janet later, all right?"

"Make sure you do. You only need a session or two so she can teach you how to *not* go off-piste to the degree you just have. There's skating close to the line, then there's jumping right over it. Jesus."

"Shut up now, I get it." George glanced around and smiled, spotting a couple of familiar green tubs on the worktop. "Make us one of them Pot Noodles, will you?"

Chapter Twenty-Three

In their normal attire, Greg felt more like himself, glad the death shenanigans were over for the time being. George doing what he had…what a knob. Whether it would be awkward seeing Janet again or not, George had to suck it up and do it, because Greg wasn't too happy about his brother going down for a long stretch if his latest move got him caught. George had eaten his Pot Noodle and messaged Janine, telling her who the skin belonged to. She'd been at the station at the time, using someone else's login to check the database, and fortunately, Pete's DNA wasn't on file, but still, George had taken a stupid risk, one of his worst ones yet.

Greg shook himself out of his bad mood and concentrated on what was going on now— finding out what had happened to Yvette so Sienna could get some closure. They sat in the back room at The Dog and Flea, Moon's 'office', a lunch of pie, mash, and liquor in front of them, steam rising. Moon sat opposite, Brickhouse beside him. Alien was off on reconnaissance, trying to catch a drug dealer red-handed.

"So," Moon said, "this is nice, although I have a feeling you're not here to sample my pub's food."

"We need to pick your brains," George said.

Moon cut into his steak pie. "What about?"

"The clinic." George scooped mash up and ate it.

"What do you need to know?" Moon asked.

George, too busy eating, nudged Greg for him to take over.

Greg obliged. "Do you know Yvette Weggley?"

"The name rings a bell." Moon frowned. "Now why do I know her?" He thought for a bit, clearly racking his brains. "Nope, it's not coming to me. The memory isn't what it used to be, I'm afraid. Jog it a bit."

"She lived on our patch, was the sister of Valerie Weggley who ran a loan shark outfit behind Cardigan's back."

Moon held his fork midair. "Ah, *now* the old brain's ticking. Yeah, Valerie, and what was her bloke's name...that fucking prick, Bear."

Greg sliced his pie in half to give it a chance to cool down. "Bear?"

"His name was Rupert, and he didn't like it. People kept calling him Rupert the Bear, see, especially because he had similar trousers, except his were lime green. They *were* chequered, though, so what did he expect? What's gone on, then, for you to be asking about that lot?"

"They apparently used the clinic. Yvette was *disposed* of."

Moon nodded. "I remember it now. It was when Cardigan ran your estate. The clinic asked for my permission to let them get rid of a body.

Yvette had done something or other, can't remember what, and she'd died. I allowed the disposal because I enjoyed the fact the Weggleys were fucking around behind Ron's back. Blame it on me being young and hating the twat, so I'd have done whatever to get one over on him, even if he didn't know it. Nowadays, I'd want to know all the ins and outs before I agreed to a disposal, that comes with wisdom, but back then, I was a bit of a dickhead. How come it's resurfaced now?"

George, who'd wolfed down his food already, despite it being surface-of-the-sun hot, filled Moon in, finishing with, "So now Sienna wants to know what happened to her mother and why."

"I can't help you there, I was just told it was an accident." He paused. "Hold up. You said Sienna. I'm sure the nipper was called Sadie."

"They changed her name. Long story."

"Who did?"

"Like I said, long story. We'll fill you in another day. What would the clinic have done with the body?"

"The fella who used to do that shit is dead, and I stopped letting that sort of thing go on after he'd snuffed it. If I remember rightly, he had a deal going on with one of the undertakers. Doubled up the coffins, if you catch my drift. Yvette would have been cremated with someone else—burial was too dodgy. Couldn't risk an exhumation for whatever reason."

"At least we know what happened to the body," Greg said, "just not *why* she was killed."

"What about speaking to that bird Yvette hung around with. Shit, what was she called in those days? Something beginning with T. A right daft name." Moon clicked his fingers. "Twinkle—and no, I'm not joking. She was a sex worker. I used her from time time—no judgement, thanks very much—and she used to live down Solomon Square, number two. Had a couple of nippers."

Greg got on with eating his food. They'd pay this Twinkle a visit, see what she had to say, and if it wasn't too much for Sienna to handle, they'd pass on the details. If it was…well, some things were better off left in the past.

Number two Solomon Square stood out from the other properties. It had clearly been bought off the council at some point and done up. The others paled in comparison. Twinkle's—if she still lived there—had new windows, a shiny front door, and a flower-riddled garden.

George knocked, and Greg braced himself to deal with a woman who might not want to remember such a terrible thing in the past, *if* she even knew about it. He'd told George to keep quiet—this needed tact, not him jumping in with both feet, getting pushy if she didn't have any answers.

A woman answered, her pixie cut not the soft, flattering kind. It stood up in hard spikes, a little like Hannah's, wet gel obvious, as if she hadn't moved on from the early nineties.

"Yeah?" she said, one skinny hip propped against the doorframe, arms folded over a navy-blue sequinned top that glittered in the sunshine.

"Twinkle?" Greg asked, wondering if her name came from her choice of clothing.

"I haven't been called that in years. What are you after? I don't do that no more."

Alarmed she thought they were there for sex, Greg elbowed George to stop him from openly laughing. "Err, we need a chat."

"The only reason you big twins would be here is if I'm in trouble. Or has one of my boys done summat?"

"Not that we're aware of. We're here about Yvette Weggley."

"Oh." Her demeanour changed, her shoulders slumping, her expression clouding over, eyes misting. "You'd better come in, then. Which one's which?"

"I'm Greg, and that's George."

She stepped back to allow them entry. "Not that I can tell the difference anyway, but still." She led them into a beige living room, lots of blingy ornaments, crystal this and mirrored glass that. "Park your arses, and I'll go and get us a drink. Coke all right? It's too hot for a cuppa."

"Yep, cheers."

They sat, George inspecting their surroundings, hunching forward on the sofa to peer at a framed photo of two blokes, probably her sons. He choked on air and pointed, flapping his hand about.

Greg leant over, and his guts twisted.

One of the men was Donkey.

"Shit," he whispered.

George flopped back. "At least that saves us trying to find his mother."

Twinkle returned and caught Greg staring at the picture. She handed the cans out. "They're my boys."

"Lovely." Greg popped the tab, hoping George kept his gob shut. They'd send her a note and money anonymously, plus they'd need to get a move on in case the police came to give her the bad news of Donkey's death. "So, we're here to find out what happened to Yvette."

"How come? It's been years."

"Her daughter came to us for help. You'd know her as Sadie."

Twinkle's eyebrows shot up. "It must have been awful growing up in care or one of them foster homes."

Why does she think Sienna did that?

Twinkle sat on an armchair. "How is she?"

"She's doing well. Is that what you think happened then, she was put in care?"

"Well, yeah, because that's what Valerie said to one of her mates before she moved away. I thought it was rotten, personally, not taking the baby in, but Valerie was a cow through and through, so it shouldn't have surprised me, and it turns out she was pregnant, so maybe that was the reason, she couldn't handle two babies. She called hers Sienna, apparently. People talk, you know."

"So they moved, eh?"

"Yeah, soon after Yvette went missing."

"Went missing?"

"Well, that's what the story was, but I think different."

"What do *you* think, then?"

"She was killed. Yvette came to me one night. She was in a right old state, you know, shaking and whatever, babbling a bit. Yvette had been...let's just say she was seeing someone she shouldn't, and Valerie didn't like it."

"Why?"

"Because in the heat of the moment, as it were, Yvette could have let it slip what Valerie and Bear were doing."

"Why would it matter if she did?"

"Because Yvette's squeeze was Sadie's father, and he wouldn't have been pleased if he got wind of what was going on."

A sense of unease crept over Greg. "Who was he?"

Twinkle settled back, her face showing her disgust. "Ron Cardigan, that's who."

George almost shot up off the sofa so he could grip Twinkle round the throat and demand answers, but Greg pressed his knee against his, halting his initial reaction.

Fuck me, Sienna's our little sister?

"Are you sure she was seeing Ron?" Greg sounded a damn sight calmer than George felt.

"Yep, he took her out nights—proper nights, Up West, all them shows and whatever. He wore disguises, mind. Anyway, Yvette got up the duff, and Ron ditched her, said she had to go and get an abortion. Obviously, she ignored him, kept out of the way for the whole pregnancy."

George imagined Yvette having to go into hiding, just so she could keep her baby.

Twinkle sighed. "She met up with Valerie one day; ooh, Sadie must have been about three months old. Yvette told her to stop playing games behind Ron's back because she'd heard he was getting suspicious about the loan business. Valerie told Yvette to go and see Ron, tell him

306

someone else's name so *they'd* get it in the neck instead. Yvette had come here in a tizzy that night, saying she didn't want to see Ron again, but her sister was forcing her into it. I told her to ignore Valerie, let her deal with it."

Another Treacle. Another pregnant woman.

George gritted his teeth, wishing Ron stood in front of him now so he could kill him over and over again. Ron had used women, discarding them when he got bored or they found themselves with a bun in the oven. Having him as their biological father was a cross they had to bear, but George wished it had been different, that someone else had fathered them, a kind man, someone who'd given a shit.

He had to know if the pattern had been the same with Yvette and asked, "Ron most have known she'd kept the baby, he'd have seen her around. It's not like you can hide a pushchair, is it. What did he do about that?"

"As far as I know, he'd told Yvette he'd deny being the father if she ever opened her mouth. He really was a bastard. So she told people she'd been raped—harsh, but she was in a panic at the time. I reckon he murdered Yvette. I think she went round to see him like Valerie wanted and it all went wrong."

It wouldn't surprise George, but not knowing all the facts was pissing him off. Who could shed some light on it? There was their older half-sister, Ron's firstborn, but they didn't have anything to do with her, and who was to say she'd even know about something like that? The spiteful bitch liked to pretend she was a cut above and that her father hadn't been a thug, so she'd be no use, the delusional cow. Sam, Ron's sidekick, was dead, but maybe Jack Pleasant from The Eagle would know, or Fiona, his wife. Jack had been well in with Ron back in the day.

"Is that all you know?" he asked.

"Yeah."

"Did you not think to report her missing?"

"No, because I'd bumped into Valerie in the supermarket, and she'd said Yvette had run away, putting her baby in care. I imagined she'd become so scared of Ron she'd legged it."

"Yet you said you thought he'd killed her."

"I do."

"So you kept it quiet in case he turned on you?"

"Yeah."

The doorbell rang, and George peered through the nets. Fuck it, the pigs were here, likely about Donkey. "You've got visitors. Plod. We weren't here, got it? We'll see ourselves out the back way."

Taking his Coke with him, George left the room, Greg following, and they jogged out of the garden into an alley. They turned left, coming to the end of the street, then walked to the BMW and got in. Drove away.

Greg clearly didn't fancy talking, but George did.

He put the can in the cup holder. "What the actual fuck?"

"I know."

"Go to The Eagle."

"Already going there. Stanley might know something."

The old man had propped the bar up for decades and knew things about their mother they hadn't necessarily wanted to know—the fact she'd been a Treacle; they were Ron's sons; she'd been forced into murder, threatened, hurt; she'd done whatever Ron had said so she stayed alive.

Ron's habit of creating emotional destruction wherever he went had far-reaching consequences. He'd fathered Gail, their other half-sister, and God knew how many others. Now there was Sienna…

That bastard has a lot to answer for.

In The Eagle, George stormed straight up to Stanley who got the gist this wasn't a social visit. His face showed his understanding, that he'd need to dig deep into his memories and come up with some answers.

"Out the back," George barked.

Jack, on the other side of the bar, came over, drying a pint glass. "What's the matter?"

"We need to use the back room," Greg said.

Jack nodded. "Go through. I'll bring some drinks in. Looks like you need them."

George led the way, barging into the back room and plonking himself down at the table, then he stood and paced, unable to keep still. His anger towards Ron Cardigan burned so bright he wanted to turn into Ruffian and take it out on someone. To kill, to stab and stab and stab until whoever had been unfortunate enough to cross his path gurgled on blood and convulsed as their life drained out of them.

Stanley shuffled in, as old as the hills, and lowered himself into a chair, his drink in hand. Greg followed, sitting beside him, and Fiona poked her head in.

"It's my chilli special today. Anyone hungry?"

"Not for us, thanks," George said, "but you know Stanley won't say no."

The old boy would take anything on offer, the tight sod.

"That'd be lovely." Stanley rubbed his hands.

Fiona left, and Jack appeared, bringing in a tray topped with glasses and half a bottle of whiskey. He placed it down and went to walk out, but George stopped him.

"Oi, you might know something, so stay."

Jack settled on a chair and poured the drinks. "What the fuck's going on?"

"Yvette Weggley," George said. "Disappeared over twenty years ago. What do you know about her, her sister, and some bloke called Rupert the Bear?"

"Valerie and Bear used to live round here before they moved away."

"Do you know where they moved to?"

"Word went round that they'd legged it because they didn't want to be right under Ron's nose. Rumour had it they were lending money without his permission. Once Ron found out it was true, and we're talking years later because they were bloody clever at hiding it, they happened to both die from an overdose a few weeks apart."

"When was this?" Greg sipped his drink.

"Before you two took over. Ron arranged it, obviously. The deaths, I mean. I thought it was a bit risky, seeing as they weren't drug-takers, but the police seemed to think it was some kind of joint suicide pact. Letters were left behind, see. Ron must have forced them to write them." Jack shook his head. "When I think about the kind of shit that went down, me knowing about it, loyal to Ron… I should never have kept his secrets, but he had a way about him, as you know. It wasn't like I could have said no."

"That's in the past," George said, "and you've already apologised before, so shut up. We're more bothered about Sienna, Yvette's daughter."

"You've got that wrong, she's Valerie's," Jack said.

"No, she used to be called Sadie. She's Yvette's—and Ron's."

"Oh, fuck me." Stanley rubbed his temples. "That man…"

George shot him a warning glare: *Don't say a word about our mum.* Stanley nodded and got on with the business of sipping his topped-up whiskey.

A knock at the door, and Fiona called out, "Can I come in?"

George opened it, took Stanley's chilli, thanked her, and closed the door. "Here." He put the food in front of the old man and addressed Jack. "So, what do you know about Yvette going missing?"

Jack sighed. "It's horrible, remembering. I've been trying to forget it all. Put some distance between me and the shit that went on so I can tell myself I had nothing to do with it."

"I get that, but it's just us lot, and we all know how Ron could persuade people to do what he wanted. Just tell us, will you?"

Jack took a swig of alcohol. Winced. "Yvette turned up here one night and spoke to Ron. I went with him and Yvette out the back—he'd asked me to go. She comes out with all this guff that it wasn't Valerie and Bear doing the money lark but some geezer called Tyke. I forget his real name. He's dead anyway, Ron got Sam to off him. So Ron asked her about an abortion, why she hadn't had one. I didn't know why it was any of his business, I didn't know the kid was his, and I just stood there, saying nothing. She said she couldn't bear to do it, and he beat her up."

Ruffian tugged at George's nerves. *Let me out, let me out.* "What did *you* do?"

"What *could* I do? You didn't go against Ron, you *know* that. He shoved her to the ground, kicked the shit out of her, even in the head, then told me to get rid of her and went back inside. I took her to Valerie's. Suggested a clinic, the one on Moon's estate, and I assume they took her there. I didn't see her after that."

Halfway through his chilli, Stanley paused. "I remember Bear coming in, later that night. Looked like death warmed over, he did. He got rat-arsed, mumbled about a coma, that a woman didn't come out of it, she'd died."

George nodded. "He'd have been thinking he couldn't let her death be known by the authorities because otherwise he'd have Ron on his back. Why the fuck go to The Eagle, though, the one place Ron was guaranteed to be? Did he have a death wish?" He finally sat. "We know the clinic disposed of her. Valerie and Bear moved to another part of the estate, taking Sadie with them. They changed her name, brought her up as if she was theirs, fake birth certificate, all of that. She's recently found out they weren't her parents, and now we've got to tell her what happened to her mother and why. Fucking hell."

"Can't you just say she died as a result of a beating and be done with it?" Jack asked.

"And how do we explain no death certificate, no grave or whatever? No, she'd know we were lying. We have to tell her the truth." George looked at Greg to check if that meant the *whole* truth, that they were related.

Greg shook his head. George nodded in return. Sensible. They didn't know Sienna well enough to trust her with that secret. Very few knew Ron had fathered them, and it needed to stay that way.

"She thinks her dad is a rapist," George said. "Do we maintain that lie?"

Jack swallowed the rest of his whiskey. "No, say you've spoken to me and I remember Yvette seeing a bloke for a while but I don't recall his name, and add that he's dead, so there's no point her looking for him."

"Right, let me get the story straight. Yvette died from a beating, Valerie and Bear arranged to get rid of the body, and there's nothing more that can be done." George downed his drink. "We'll look after her from the sidelines."

Greg stood, leaving his booze unfinished. "Come on, let's go and break the news."

Chapter Twenty-Four

A three-sided tent had been erected, the open edge against a fir tree. Janine bent in front of the body, strips of skin just visible inside the mouth. What did they mean, and why were they there? What was George's reasoning? She hadn't had a chance to ask him earlier because she'd left the station to visit Sienna Weggley, going with Colin to inform her of the death of her sister.

George had admitted the strips belonged to Pete, though, and thank God his DNA wasn't on file.

The photos had been taken, Jim had done all of his initial checks, and he'd crouched to dig inside the victim's pocket in the hopes of finding ID. "Ah, a wallet." He'd opened it and slid out a driver's licence. "Tanner Vardy. Number two Solomon Square."

Janine thought back to when George had said they'd had Donkey's—Tanner's—place under surveillance. They hadn't mentioned that he lived with his mother, so maybe the licence hadn't been updated. She'd sent uniforms round for the death knock instead of doing it herself. She didn't fancy another of those today.

"I've already done Hannah's PM," Jim said now. "Cause of death, bullet to the head. The stomach wounds were from a knife with a blade of approximately eight inches. Once the blood was cleaned off, she had bruising, which indicated the stabs were done with force. The bruises are in the shape of the knife handle edge that's closest to the blade, which is called a bolster; something to tuck into your 'You learn something new every day' folder."

"Err, thanks?"

Jim nodded. "You're welcome. Whoever did that to her was angry. Understandable, given that she'd killed a child. Any leads on who her killer is yet? And this chap's, I suspect, although he hasn't been stabbed. The skin in the mouth tells me it's likely to be the same person, though."

"No leads," she said, "although I want Dillon Nivens to account for his whereabouts. It could have been him, proving my point that he knew damn well who'd come to his door. Whoever killed Hannah and Tanner knew them, or at least knew where they'd be in order to kill them. I've got people out asking questions. Her sister, Sienna, said Hannah didn't have any friends but she spent a lot of time with a man—I assume that's this bloke. As far as Sienna's concerned, although they lived next door to each other, they weren't close. She was shocked about the murder, obviously, and that Hannah had killed Libby, but couldn't offer anything that would forward the investigation."

"I'll get that skin sent down to the lab as soon as possible to see if it matches what was left in Hannah's mouth. I asked for that to be rushed through for you, by the way."

"Thanks, I appreciate that." She already knew there wasn't a DNA match in the database but would play the disheartened copper when the second skin results came back.

"I find it odd that the skin doesn't belong to the victims—odd that it was even put in their mouths in the first place." Jim sniffed.

"Who knows what goes on inside people's heads. We may never find out the reason. Right, is there anything of relevance you can tell me that will help with the investigation? I need to drop round to the Nivens' place to let them know this fella's been found."

"Nothing's standing out to me at the moment. Standard execution."

"Okay. Well, try and have a good day."

She left the tent and switched her booties out, placed them in a bag, and put new ones on to walk to the cordon. She removed her protectives, gave them to a nearby officer, and signed out of the log. Colin had already done so; he sat waiting in the car, drinking Pepsi Max. She joined him, pulling the tab of her can, sipping while contemplating her next move.

"We'll nip to see Libby's parents then go and see Tanner Vardy's next of kin. She'll have

320

already been given the news so will have calmed down a bit."

Colin fished out his notebook. "DC Owen gave me some details."

"Right. Any other relatives?"

Colin nodded. "A brother. According to the database, the pair of them have been arrested before."

"Lovely. So are we walking into a potential minefield when it comes to how they perceive the police? Are they angry types?"

"Dunno."

"Actually, I've changed my mind. We'll go and visit Mrs Vardy now, see if she can give me ammo to throw at Nivens." She drove off. "I want to see if he's going to finally admit why Hannah and Tanner were at his door, and Tanner's mother might be able to shed some light on that."

Colin slurped his Pepsi all the way there, and she resisted telling him to pack it in. If all he had were irritating habits, she'd be grateful, as he was the perfect partner otherwise. She parked behind a patrol car, and they got out. At the door, Janine took a deep breath then knocked.

A PC answered, one she'd seen before but had forgotten his name, and he let them in, pulling a face to warn them that it had been tough going for whatever reason. Could be the mother had crumbled, or she'd become irate, or wasn't being cooperative.

In the living room, Janine nodded for the officers to leave, they'd done their bit, and sat beside Mrs Vardy, Colin gratefully lowering his arse into a comfy-looking armchair, squashing the perfectly plumped pillows.

"I'm DI Janine Sheldon. I'm sorry for your loss." *I'm not really, he was scum.*

Spiky-haired Mrs Vardy rubbed at her nose with a scrunched tissue. "I should have known he'd come a cropper one day."

"What do you mean?"

"He was hanging around with that bloody Hannah, the one who was on the news this morning. She killed that little girl, didn't she?"

Janine grimaced at that snippet getting out. Only someone from the investigation would have known Hannah was responsible, so someone had leaked the information. "We're assuming that, yes. Do you know why Tanner would have been involved in that?"

"He was her bodyguard, that's what he told me. She carried a lot of money round with her so needed him for protection. Like mother like daughter." She grunted in disgust.

Janine feigned ignorance so Colin didn't get suss. "Why would she have money on her, enough that she'd need a bodyguard?"

"She was a lender. Her and her sister."

Janine had to shut that train down before it even left the station. "No, her sister wasn't involved. We've already spoken to her."

"She could just be saying that."

Janine gritted her teeth. *This* was why she got arsey at the twins for putting her in these situations. She had to think on her feet a lot. "Hannah used to tell people her sister was in the lending business with her, but in reality, she hardly had anything to do with her."

"I wasn't surprised Hannah turned out nasty."

"Did you know her, then?"

"No, but I knew her parents. My friend was Hannah's aunt."

Janine didn't need this shit being brought up. "Let's go back to your son."

Mrs Vardy smiled through her tears. "He was such a donkey as a kid. That's what we called him, Donkey. I don't know what went wrong. Maybe it was his dad dying. Neither of my boys were the same after that. They kept getting into trouble, got arrested a couple of times. But I never expected…expected this. What was he thinking, going with her to that house? I told him not to get involved with the Weggleys, that they weren't to be trusted. She *did* kill the girl, didn't she? Please don't tell me it was him."

"Going by witness statement, it was her, yes."

"It had to be something to do with lending money. I bet that little girl's parents borrowed some."

That was exactly what Janine needed to hear. She now had the green light to question Dillon Nivens about it; previous to this, she'd had to act as if she didn't know why Hannah and Tanner had been to the house. She glanced at Colin and raised her eyebrows. He cottoned on to why and smiled.

"I think Tanner got caught up in something he couldn't get out of," Janine said to make the woman feel better. "I bet we'll find that to be the case as the investigation progresses. Is there anyone we can phone to sit with you? Your other son, perhaps?"

Mrs Vardy nodded. "He's on his way. The other coppers got hold of him for me." She paused, head cocked. "That sounds like his car now. Dodgy exhaust."

"We'll leave you be, then." Janine stood and flicked her hand about to get Colin to do the same. She wanted to get out of here quickly. "I'll be your point of contact, okay?" She handed over her card. "Anything you need to talk about, you ring me, no one else. I'll let you know when you can view your son's body, and I'll tell you any pertinent information, but from what I can gather, honestly, your son was with the wrong person at the wrong time, and that's *all*."

"Thank you. That makes me feel better."

The scrape of a key in the lock, then, "Mum?"

Janine walked out, nodded to the other son in the hallway, and left the house. In the car, desperate to message The Brothers, she had to keep her irritation at bay while she drove to the station, Colin slurping the remainder of his can.

In the incident room, she got on with pretending to properly lead the case. "Right, team, as far as I've gathered, Tanner Vardy was with Hannah Weggley but was just her bodyguard; she carried a lot of cash on her, and he was her protection. There's a gun at his scene, and we'll soon see if his prints are on it. If not, and hers are, then we know what's what. Get back to work on CCTV and ANPR. We need to find two vehicles." She rattled off the number plates of the two burnt-out cars left in the woods. "I'm not hopeful of getting an image of the driver, whoever it is likely knows this part of London inside out so avoided the cameras, but you never know."

She prayed nothing would be found but had to play the part of the good copper. In time, this investigation would go cold. Until then, she had a role to fulfil.

As the twins' bitch.

Her burner phone vibrated, and she rushed into her office to answer it.

The information she received from SOCO about a notebook had her smiling wide. Now she could use the information the twins had given her. Brilliant.

Dillon Nivens stared at Janine with fear in his eyes. His wife, Lesley, sat beside him, focusing on the patterned carpet.

"A second body has been found," Janine said from her position standing by the living room doorway. She wanted the upper hand here, and looking down on someone was the perfect way to make them feel inferior and out of sorts. "I had another anonymous call, stating that the body was the man who was with Hannah Weggley. His name is Tanner Vardy, also known as Donkey. Do you know him?"

Dillon shook his head. "No."

"I'm going to give you the opportunity, one more time, to admit that you do. Certain information has come to light... Do you know him?"

"No, I swear." He used his eyes to plead with her, to beg her not to get him in the shit.

Janine didn't care. She wanted him to suffer because he'd been prepared, and still was, to hide pertinent information despite his daughter being killed. He was a wanker for doing that, the worst kind of person.

"Okay, have it your way. We know Hannah was a money lender. We know Tanner worked for her as a bodyguard. We *also* know your name is in a notebook at her flat and that you borrowed ten thousand pounds. Can you explain how you don't know her despite that evidence?"

"I have no idea why my name would be in that book."

Lesley stared at him. "*Ten* thousand pounds? What the hell would you need to borrow that for?"

"I didn't, Les!"

"So how was your name in her book? It's not like Dillon is common, is it?" Lesley whittled her fingers, although that might be to stop herself from strangling him, because her face displayed her anger and suspicion.

"Would you like me to say what else was in that book?" Janine asked. "Or would you prefer to admit it yourself, Mr Nivens? It's just that I understand you might not want your wife to know what you spent the money on, but in the face of your little girl's death, I'd have thought you'd have felt finding her killer was more important than hiding your secret."

"What secret?" Lesley gritted out.

Tension grew, the air uncomfortable with it. Janine was prepared to let the silence stretch. People tended to want to fill the gap with words instead of having all eyes on them.

"I didn't mean it," Dillon said. "I couldn't help it."

"Couldn't help what?" his wife asked. "What could be so terrible that you'd want to keep it from the police, from me, when the most terrible thing has already happened to us? What could be worse than Libby dying? What?"

Exactly how Janine felt. "Mr Nivens? Your behaviour is called perverting the course of justice, and you could be punished for it. You have deliberately withheld information, preventing us from finding the killer and her bodyguard. If you'd have admitted to knowing them, we would have arrested them. Instead, someone has found them first and killed them, and now they won't pay for what they've done. They won't go to prison and serve time for taking Libby's life, which is what *should* have happened."

He stared at her, mute.

She'd soon get him talking again. "Where were you between the hours of ten p.m. yesterday and seven a.m. this morning?"

"What? You think *I* killed them?"

"It's not implausible. You could have done it to hide your secret."

Lesley rose and stamped her foot. "*What* bloody secret?"

"Oh, Jesus Christ…" Dillon put his face in his hands and sobbed. "I was home last night, Lesley will tell you."

"And your secret is…?" Janine held back a smirk.

He dropped his hands and studied the fireplace opposite. "I used it for escorts."

"What?" Lesley clenched her fists at her sides. "You had sex with women and thought it was okay to hide that from the police? What is *wrong* with you? No matter what you've done, you should have said something, on the quiet if necessary."

"But you'd have found out in court!"

Lesley scoffed. "None of that matters anymore. I knew you were playing away, so it wouldn't have been news to me. Fucking *hell*, Dillon, what kind of father *are* you?" She rushed out in tears, her feet thudding on the stairs.

"Happy now?" Dillon asked.

"Yes, thank you." Janine strode out, hoping Lesley left him. Hoping he'd be unhappy for the rest of his life, alone, no one to call his own.

Men like him deserved all they got. If he'd thought more about finding the killers than hiding his bullshit, Janine wouldn't have two more bodies on her hands. She wouldn't have such a mess to deal with.

Fucking prick.

In the car, she waited for Colin who must have scarpered after her because he was in the passenger seat in a flash.

"You didn't tell me about the escorts," he said.

She smiled. "I thought you wanted the easy life at work."

"I know, but *that* kind of juicy gossip…"

They chuckled all the way back to the station.

Chapter Twenty-Five

Two days after The Brothers had told her the story about her real mother, Sienna left Twinkle's house knowing more about Yvette than anyone had ever told her before. Now she had a better image of her. Sienna had maintained the ruse she was Yvette's niece, so no awkward questions were asked. According to Twinkle, Yvette had been kind and funny, a joy to be around. George and Greg had warned Sienna that Twinkle was Donkey's mum, and it had been awkward as hell, giving her condolences.

She owed the twins now, they'd spared her life, and she was a part of their 'family' as they'd put it, meaning they'd set her up in a new flat, get her legitimate loan business set up, and they'd look after her.

It had been nice of Twinkle to see her when she was going through so much grief. She'd said it was okay, it'd take her mind off her son being murdered and linked to the death of that poor little girl. All the same, Sienna had battled guilt, being selfish in pushing for any snippet of information she could about her real mother.

It was time to do what George and Greg had said. Move on. The past didn't do you any favours, did it, just haunted you day and night, delivering bouts of anxiety that had no business infiltrating the present.

Knowing Yvette had died as a result of a beating had been hard to take, and the fact that Valerie and Bear had covered it up, all because they didn't want attention drawn to their business, was a bitter pill to swallow. Sick, the pair of them. Yvette had been cremated, so at least she'd been put to rest somewhere, although the twins hadn't been able to find out where her ashes had ended up.

As for her father... Twinkle had said she didn't know who he was. Via The Brothers, Sienna was relieved to know Yvette hadn't been raped, that she'd had a good relationship with a man and, for whatever reason, they'd parted ways. Sienna had spoken to Jack at The Eagle, and he'd assured her Yvette had been happy during her pregnancy but unfortunately, he couldn't remember Sienna's father's name, so she couldn't look up other family members and introduce herself as a long-lost relative.

Maybe that was for the best. Sienna didn't need family, especially the type she'd been used to. A nasty, crazy mum and dad and a so-called sister who'd terrorised her in their childhood and controlled her as an adult. A nasty 'uncle' who'd hurt her for pleasure.

She was better off alone.

She got in her car, a new one since she'd sold hers which had been used as a getaway vehicle in Libby's murder. The twins had found her a two-seater sports car, saying it was a welcome-to-the-fold gift. It seemed a bit extravagant, but she wasn't going to look those gift horses in the mouth. They were a strange pair, menacing and scary, yet they couldn't do enough for her, checking up via phone calls and WhatsApp, seeing if she was okay.

Was this what being in a proper family was like?

She drove away, imagining Yvette, how happy she'd been when Sienna was born. Twinkle had said Yvette's daughter was much loved, the apple of her mother's eye, and if Sienna took anything away with her from all of this, it was to know the child was wanted, adored. Twinkle had handed photos over of Yvette at parties, and they were tucked in Sienna's handbag, ready to be pulled out later. She'd studied them already, spotted the resemblances between them, their hair colour the exact same shade, their noses with the same slope.

If only she'd known her. The ache in her chest over that hurt, so she switched her mind to better things, like the stories Twinkle had told her. Yvette blowing raspberries on Sienna's tummy; the way she'd held her to her chest after a feed; the lullabies she used to sing.

Sienna would cherish those until her dying day.

They were all she had.

And her real name. Sadie.

Chapter Twenty-Six

George stood in Zoe's kitchen and hoped he wouldn't get an ear-bashing. It had been a hectic few days, and he wanted to tie this saga up with a nice big bow and move on, although he had a couple of little jobs to do in a bit. Greg reckoned Zoe would be okay, but there was always that worry someone wouldn't take the news well, even though they were aware it was coming at some point.

"You know I promised to wait until he'd been dealt with before we told you about Pete..." George started.

She eyed him, her face falling. "Oh. It's done, is it?"

"Hmm. He won't be bothering you again. Ever."

"As in, he's agreed to leave us alone or...?"

"Or."

"Right. So you went for killing him over a knee-capping." She sat at her table and stared outside into the garden. "I don't know how I'm supposed to feel."

"Relieved? He's given you grief for a fair while now, and with him nicking your holiday fund, he clearly didn't give a shit about you all."

"Say it how you see it, why don't you."

"Better than me bullshitting. He was a waste of space, and you're better off without him."

"What did you do with the body?"

"It won't turn up, if that's what you're worried about."

"What do I need to tell my boys?"

"That you don't know where he is and he must have moved away."

"Fine."

She swiped at a tear, maybe for the man she thought Pete had been when she'd first met him, maybe because she didn't have to live on tenterhooks anymore. Whatever the reason, they'd got rid of him, and he wouldn't be wreaking havoc again.

"What about Genevieve?" she asked.

"She'll be all right." George told her what had happened at Genevieve's flat and why Pete had to be sorted quickly. "You're both well shot of him."

Instead of tackling this in secret, George had admitted he was off to do a little job by himself. Greg had agreed to be the getaway driver, although he was none too happy about it, pointing out all the pitfalls—pitfalls George had already contemplated.

In a blond beard and wig, he stood in the trendy reception area of The Elms care home, waiting for the nurse to return. He'd introduced himself as Abel's nephew, Ben, who existed but hadn't ever met his uncle. The PI, Mason, had emailed a lot more information, and George was using it to his advantage.

Nurse King came back, all smiles. "Yes, he remembers his sister had a son, and your ID checks out, so he's happy to see you. He doesn't get many visitors, just his two nieces, although they haven't been for a while."

That must be Hannah and Sienna.

"Brilliant," he said. "Since my mum died, I've been wanting to connect with family members. You know how it is. When you've got no one close left, you root round to see if there are people you didn't know about."

"It'll be nice for you to catch up, although I'll warn you, he's a grumpy bugger at times. This way."

She walked off down a corridor, and George followed. He had gloves in his suit pocket, plus his tools for the job. Their dodgy doctor had explained about an air injection and the effects of it. A simple way to dispatch the old bastard. George had worried someone in the care home would get the blame for murder once a post-mortem had discovered the cause of death, but no, they'd remember the big blond man with the Welsh accent, the name he'd given, and the investigation would swing to Cardiff and finding that naughty nephew, Ben. It would soon become clear Ben hadn't done it, but for now, it would keep the police busy.

George didn't intend on getting caught anyway. He had his escape route all mapped out. He'd walked here over the fields, and he'd go back the same way, only needing to go as far as the country road where Greg, in a stolen car, waited to pick him up.

Nurse King stopped at a door and tapped on it, then poked her head round. She turned to George. "Ah, he's fallen asleep. He does that a lot. It's the medication."

"Doesn't matter. I can sit with him for a bit, and if it doesn't look like he'll wake up, I can come back another day."

"Fair enough." She pushed the door wide.

George went inside, praying she didn't hang around, and sat on the chair beside the one Abel snoozed in. He glanced at King, forcing his eyes to water. "He looks just like my mum."

"Bless you. It's a bit emotional, isn't it?"

"Yeah." He cleared his throat. "I'll be all right, though."

"If you want a cuppa, just press the buzzer there." She retreated and closed the door.

George blinked the fake tears away, snapped his gloves on, and mulled over what he was doing. This was a dangerous game, being here. He'd clocked the CCTV, in reception, although there wasn't any in this room, not unless the cameras were hidden. This job was high-risk, and Greg had chewed his arse over it, saying this was one person they didn't need to kill, because he'd be dead soon all by himself.

George had brushed his concerns aside. This bastard had cut Sienna for no other reason that it was a warped predilection, he'd done it for kicks, and it wasn't acceptable.

He got up and stood over Abel, bending double. He didn't feel the need to wake the fucker up and let him know what was coming, not in this situation. The less fuss the better.

He turned Abel's arm over and did what he'd been instructed, using a torniquet to plump the veins then inserting the needle and releasing the rubber band. The man didn't even stir. What the fuck meds was he *on*? He watched Abel for a moment or two, recalling what their doctor had said.

"It'll cause a cerebral embolism. Two to three millilitres of air will kill him. Cardiac arrest."

George had inserted five. It was happening now, Abel waking, his eyes wide, his heart on the way to giving up the ghost. George smiled, tucked the syringe and torniquet away, and walked out. He closed the door, popped his gloves away, and strolled through reception casually.

"Oh, going so soon?" King called from beside a flower display.

He spun and faced her. "He's snoring, so I doubt he's going to wake up anytime soon. I'm staying at a hotel not far from here. I'll be back tomorrow." He'd slipped into Ruffian's Scottish accent for the word 'hotel' —*fuck*—and waited to see if she'd noticed.

Was she eyeing him funny? He didn't want to have to get shirty and deal with her in *that* way. Ask to speak to her in a private side room. Warn her not to say a word. Admit he was a Brother and she'd do well to keep her fucking mouth shut. She seemed a nice enough sort, and if she'd just leave him alone…

"Hmm, he had his cocktail about half an hour ago," she said.

"Blimey, he's living it up here, then."

She trilled out a laugh. Did she fancy him or something? If he hadn't sworn himself off women, she might well have been his type once upon a time.

"Not that kind of cocktail," she said. "Well, I must get on." She smiled and swished off in the other direction, down a different corridor.

George winked at the receptionist who admired him from behind the desk. She'd remember his vivid blue eyes courtesy of contacts, his neat beard, his carefully styled wig, his sculpted blond eyebrows.

"I wouldn't mind a cocktail if you're asking," she said.

Jesus Christ. He held up one hand to show off a ring he'd bought in a tat shop. "Married."

"Shame."

He strode out, shuddering at the predatory nature of the woman, and took a deep breath. He ambled along the front of the building. A quick glance into Abel's room showed him the man had fallen out of his chair during that heart attack and lay on the floor, his eyes staring, spit coating his mouth.

"Rot in Hell, you fucking old cunt," George muttered and headed for the fields, laughing quietly at a job well done. Within the hour, he'd have torched the lock-up, too, then this bullshit could finally be put to bed.

He hadn't expected to be sitting in Janet's office again, but here he was, later that day, taking in her smirk and hating it.

"I knew you'd still need me," she said.

"For therapy, like it used to be. None of this trying to fix me shit. I just want to do that thing where you get me to close my eyes and walk down steps, then onto a beach. I found that curbed my impulses a bit, gave me a chance to think without all the crap that fills my head."

"You could do that for yourself at home."

"But I wouldn't, you *know* that."

"Okay. Settle back, then."

He did, glad he didn't have to see 'I told you so' written in her eyes. "Any bollocks, and I'll just fuck off out of here, got it?"

"Yes, George."

"Good. Glad we're on the same wavelength."

Chapter Twenty-Seven

Janet felt smug, although she shouldn't. The only reason George had come back to her was he probably didn't want to go through all the palaver of getting to know a new therapist and the therapist getting to know him. He'd already done the hard work with her, knew she wouldn't reveal his secrets, but with someone else, he wouldn't be so sure.

He was using her, which stung. She wished he still loved her—if he ever had—and that she'd had a chance to explain to him who she really was so they could be Bonnie and Clyde together. How she was like him inside, she just hid it exceptionally well.

She put on her professional head and told herself that as long as he paid her, nothing else mattered. Except it still did. She hated not being able to fix her clients, and George wasn't someone who was willing to let her wipe the slate clean for him. She'd failed to mend her own issues, hadn't been able to get rid of the blemishes from her past, although blemishes was putting it mildly. She'd promised herself if she could heal other people, that would have to be enough. Her success rate was pretty good.

Look at Sienna. She's already changed so much since her first session.

All right, George and Greg had a lot to do with that, they'd not only wiped the slate clean but had set her up in a legitimate business, kitted her office out, bought her a car, and installed her in a fancy new flat.

Was there more to that?

None of my business.

Janet concentrated on taking George to what she called The Place of Stillness, where everything from daily life, the past, the worries that lurked in the future, all disappeared for a short while. There, she could ask him to take any route he wanted to, and while he had the choice to back out or refuse to go where she felt he needed to go, it would be better for him if he followed her guidance.

"I want you to continue along the beach until you can either carry on up the path you've chosen or take a left into the dunes. As you know, the dunes represent a place you can sit and contemplate what you need my help with. Taking the edge off, curbing those impulses you know will get you into trouble one day. What have you chosen?"

"The dunes."

"Good."

She went through the motions on autopilot, leaving him to ponder a few things for himself, and floated to her own dune, possibly contemplating the same thing as George. How to stop herself, day after day, trying not to lose her temper and kill someone.

George wasn't unique. Other people had a mad side they struggled to control.

Janet should know. She was one of them.

To be continued in *Rewrite*,
The Cardigan Estate 19

Printed in Great Britain
by Amazon

24175420R00202